Carroll Multz

The
Chameleon

A Novel

BRASS FROG BOOKWORKS™
Independent Publishers
Grand Junction, CO

Other titles by Carroll Multz

The Devil's Scribe– Nadine Siena has risen from her humble beginnings as an orphan to earn the Pulitzer Prize for journalism. When an anonymous source contacts her with a story lead, she gets embroiled in a scandal that has already cost one life and threatens to bring the town of Pembrooke to its knees. As Siena fights to protect her source, a journalist from the rival newspaper begins a treacherous campaign that threatens to destroy Nadine's career and the newspaper for which she works. As the situation quickly unravels and the attorneys face off, no one can believe the final outcome or the swift, sure destructive power of the pen.

License to Convict– Morrey Dexter wasn't used to losing. As a district attorney in Paraiso County, Colorado, Morrey owned the courtroom. He was dauntless in his quest to seek justice, committed to his sense of fairness and vigilant in his role as a protector of the community. But, when a surprising verdict shakes his faith in the system, he begins to see that things are not as simple as they appear. Can Morrey use his license to convict to preserve the things he holds sacred?

The CHAMELEON

Deadly Deception– Everywhere he looks Harvard grad and former golden boy from the district attorney's office sees Joy's piercing turquoise eyes. He tries to end their affair and things spin wildly out of control. There is a horrible accident and Joy is dead. Now Drew Quinlin is drawn into the biggest case of his career defending the person charged with her death–her husband. Will winning an acquittal appease his tortured conscience or will judgment come before he can atone for his crime?

Justice Denied– Max has come home to help. His father, Jamie Cooper, a devoted dad and faithful employee is accused of stealing $30,000 from the bank where he worked. He hires a defense team and fights to clear his name, but will that be enough to battle the combined strength of the town's powerful chief of police, a man who has held a grudge against the Cooper family for years?

Shades of Innocence– Crimson and Jade may be identical twins, but they embody the ancient belief embraced by their Chinese parents regarding the positive and negative forces in the universe. Crimson has lost her faith as she awaits execution for a murder she did not commit. All of her options have been exhausted and for her there is no hope. She bravely faces the inevitable. It is the ultimate betrayal. Then in a strange twist of fate, with only days left before her execution, the mysterious forces come together for one last time. It is her last act of giving. What alchemy will it conjure? Can redemption come from darkness?

The Chameleon
Copyright © 2013 by Carroll Multz. All rights reserved.

Published by BRASS FROG BOOKWORKS | an Independent Publishing Firm
2695 Patterson Rd. Unit 2-#168 | Grand Junction, Colorado 81506
909/239-0344 or 970/434-9361 | www.BrassFrogBookworks.com
Brass Frog Bookworks is dedicated to excellence and integrity in the publishing industry. The company was founded on the belief in the power of language and the spiritual nature of human creativity. *"In the beginning was the Word…"* John 1:1
Inquiries should be addressed to:
Carroll Multz
589 Quail Run Dr.
Grand Junction, CO 81505

Printed in the United States of America | First Printing 2013
Library of Congress Control Number:
ISBN: 978-0-9857191-5-9
Book design copyright © 2013 by Brass Frog Bookworks
Cover & Interior Design: JL Leon
www.ClickCreativeMedia.com
1.   Fiction/Legal 2.   Fiction/Suspense 3.   Fiction/Romance
Set in 11 pt. Garamond

CARROLL MULTZ

DEDICATION

This book is dedicated to Harold Moss, a former FBI agent, retired judge and cherished friend. It is also dedicated to law enforcement officers everywhere who serve and protect, and who risk their own safety to secure the safety of others.

Table of Contents

The CHAMELEON

ACKNOWLEDGEMENTS

In the midst of writing this novel, I was invited to dine at the Carrs' residence. Gary is a fellow author and he and his wife Shirley are well traveled and always have a lot of fascinating stories to tell, especially about the various foods around the world. Their particular favorite is Italian food. To them I am most grateful for the menu provided for the wedding feast at Tahoe (Chapter 26) and for instilling in me a greater appreciation for Italian and Sicilian cuisine and the specialty wines that are an integral part of every meal.

As with the other novels, I would be unable to survive without a skillful and devoted support staff. My deepest appreciation to Sherri Davis, Amber Burnell, Judy Blevins, and my daughters, Lisa Knudsen and Natalie Lowery.

My gratitude also to my sister Marilynn Kuenzi, now deceased, my nephew David Kuenzi and his wife Patrice for the tours of Chicago and to Dennis Eichinger and Erickson Nystrom for their reflections on survival in the nation's third largest city.

As always, my special thanks to my editors Patti Hoff and Jan Weeks and the exceptional staff at Brass Frog Bookworks for their dedicated attention to my publications.

Last but not least, my apologies in advance to the citizens of California, Colorado, Florida, Illinois, Nevada and New York for the literary license taken with respect to the geography of their respective states. And, to the citizens of Colorado, for the expansive application of the felony murder rule, *mea culpa, mea culpa, mea maxima culpa!*

This above all: To thine own self be true.
And it must follow, as the night the day,
Thou canst not then be false to any man.

Shakespeare

INTRODUCTION

An undercover operation is a deadly game wherein the undercover officer constantly flirts with fate. It has been said that a cat has nine lives. Depending on the nature of the stings and the alignment of the stars, the undercover officer might not be lucky enough to have that many.

This novel was inspired by the stealth of the undercover officers with whom I have come in contact during my many years as a prosecutor. Of particular note is a former agent who I had dubbed, and still fondly refer to as, The Chameleon. Others called him The Great Imposter. Early in my career, I had the honor to conduct the first state-wide grand jury that convened in Colorado. The Chameleon's artful impersonations resulted in the return of almost fifty indictments against various targets including several public officials.

The Chameleon literally had the ability to "change his colors" through contrived tattooing, his dress and the assistance of a crafty makeup artist. So convincing were his guises that he managed to out-con the cons. He reputedly

1

borrowed a page or two from Harry Houdini in making some rather spectacular and improbable escapes while in the line of duty. The only predictable things about him were his unpredictability and his unflinching courage in the face of danger. His success rate was unrivaled in the trade.

Although *The Chameleon* is a work of fiction, as the characters in this story never existed and the events never occurred, they do offer some realistic insight into the lives of those who assume an identity different from their own and who are choreographed in roles designed to solve crime and seek justice.

My lawyer father, in alerting me on the down side of the legal profession, preached to me on what later became an obvious truism: The law is a jealous mistress. However, I found that this applies to a lot of professions and occupations, including law enforcement. In this novel, the reader will get a glimpse of the impact the three Ds (the demands, dedication and disappointments) has on undercover officers and their loved ones. Hopefully, the respect and admiration I have for undercover officers will be mirrored by the reader by book's end.

CARROLL MULTZ

PROLOGUE

The Chameleon braced himself against the sway of the car as it took the curves in Clear Creek Canyon, just west of Denver, faster than was wise. He reached up to wipe a trickle of blood from the slash across his throat. Sagibaro had been meticulous with the blade, dragging it deep enough to draw blood but not deep enough to kill. That privilege was reserved for Twitch.

"Bull! Put out that damn cigarette or open the frickin' window," Twitch demanded from the back seat where he sat next to the Chameleon. His well-rehearsed hands deftly loaded the .40 Glock semiautomatic he held.

The driver reached to adjust the rearview mirror and glared at the reflection. "Hey, don't point that damn thing in my direction. You're making me nervous."

Twitch slammed the clip home with the butt of his hand and waved the gun around.

4

"Don't worry. I never shot anybody—accidentally, that is." He grinned at the Chameleon, amused by his own joke.

The Chameleon looked at him and stared into eyes as dark as death. On this first day of autumn, he knew he'd never see the next, unless he got incredibly lucky. As an undercover cop, he'd faced death many times, but never as surely as he did now. Figuring he had nothing to lose, he spoke to Bull in a listless tone. "Bull, please. Can you just crack the window a little?"

The driver guffawed. "What's the diff if you get smoked now or later?" He threw back his head and laughed.

Twitch joined in the laughter as he popped two more white pills from a vial in his jacket pocket. That made half a dozen he'd downed since they'd left Denver.

Early morning sun peeked over the ridge above the canyon where Clear Creek churned cold and quick far below on the left side of the road. Twitch and Bull lapsed into silence, giving the Chameleon time to reflect on his predicament. Six months ago, he'd successfully infiltrated the Sagibaro crime family, headed by Marcus

Sagibaro. The family was notorious, even among the most infamous criminals, for its role in bringing drugs and sex slaves from points south of the border. The Chameleon had seen the results of both trades first hand. Girls hardly into their teens were abducted, beaten and tortured, then turned over to pimps to be sold over and over— sometimes two dozen times a day—to whomever paid the price. He had seen the meth and cocaine users, cold as stone on morgue slabs, some clad in torn jeans and some in Armani slacks. The addiction makes no distinction between class or gender.

Then the unthinkable happened. One of Sagibaro's observant henchmen had spotted the transponder the Chameleon had planted on the undercarriage of Sagibaro's limo. He could have bluffed his way out when confronted, but a similar device in the pocket of his sweat pants at the bottom of his gym bag couldn't be explained away.

"Traitor!" Sagibaro had raged as three thugs lashed the Chameleon to a chair. The don's fists took revenge on the Chameleon's face and body while the others looked on, grinning and waiting for their turns to punish. The Chameleon's strength waned as he sagged against the ropes. Twitch grabbed a handful of hair and roughly jerked him upright.

Sagibaro flicked open a knife and held it menacingly close. The Chameleon watched the curved blade glint in the light and closed his eyes, hoping the end would be swift. He felt the blade decisively slash across his throat. The cut through his flesh felt hot. It was followed by the eruption of warm blood gushing from the wound and running down his chest.

Sagibaro stepped back and cocked his head to the side as if admiring the efficiency of his work. "Bull, you and Twitch take him out to our favorite cemetery."

With his hands bound behind his back, he was jerked from the chair and roughly escorted to the car waiting outside. After being jammed inside, the Chameleon found himself on his way to an old abandoned mine shaft in the mountains where other victims of Sagibaro had been taken. There, after being tortured or shot, the victims would be thrown into the shaft for a long fall into oblivion.

They had driven for some time when Bull

suddenly sat erect and rigid behind the wheel. He slowed the car to a crawl as they approached a series of orange traffic cones and a fleet of heavy equipment working just ahead.

"Uh-oh, trouble," Bull said, flicking his cigarette out the window. "Be cool," he whispered to Twitch without looking back. If our friend so much as flinches, cut out his liver."

The Chameleon jumped as Twitch roughly cut his hands free and shoved the Glock into his ribs. He looked out the tinted window at the road construction just ahead where a flagger was waving them to a stop. The Chameleon's mind raced as the young man approached, lifting the brim of his hardhat and wiping sweat from his forehead. He planted the two-way sign into the dirt and leaned toward the car. One stupid move and the man could start a blood bath.

"Had a rock fall last night," he explained while adjusting his hard hat. "Be about ten minutes before we can let you through." He nodded and walked back to the cars beginning to queue behind them.

The Chameleon allowed himself to relax a fraction. A reprieve was a reprieve, no matter the cause. And it gave him time to come up with Plan

B. While the others were intent on watching for the flagger's signal to proceed, The Chameleon surreptitiously began to undo the clasp of his belt. His movements were slow and deliberate.

Twitch unfastened his seat belt. "I gotta take a whiz. Don't make a move," he warned as he opened the door. He shoved the Glock into his waistband under his jacket and got out. Ignoring the people in the car behind them, he unzipped and let a stream wet the shoulder of the road. He never took his eyes off the Chameleon. He got back in and sighed with relief, then took out the gun again. "Good boy," he taunted, waving the barrel in the Chameleon's direction before transferring it to the other hand.

As the flagman waved them on, Bull said, "You coulda made a move back there."

The Chameleon shrugged. "Coulda had a lot of people die. For what?"

Twitch coughed and shoved the Glock under his thigh, then shook a couple more pills out of the vial. "You're making our job easy, Vinnie."

"You guys are just doing your job. Now, maybe I can make believers out of the two of you.

The CHAMELEON

Whoever fingered me was trying to divert attention away from himself. Do you think I would be *stupid* enough to plant transponders everywhere?"

Twitch leaned back against the seat, a drowsy smile on his lips. "Doesn't matter. Marcus gave the order and I gotta carry it out. He's my brother-in-law and I don't screw with family. Either one."

The swaying car and the Chameleon's lack of effort to escape lulled the other two into a state of temporary complacency. It would take at least another hour to reach their destination. Bull, a chain smoker, lit another cigarette. Twitch's eyes closed. Thankfully, he had forgotten to tie the Chameleon's hands.

The Chameleon slowly eased his belt out of the pant loops and hid it between his thighs. He waited for just the right moment. They had gone on for another dozen miles when the car entered a broad curve. Twitch was snoring and Bull was struggling to light yet another cigarette while steering with his elbow. He cursed as the cigarette fell into his lap, and he tried to retrieve it. The Chameleon saw his chance. Lunging forward, he looped the belt around Bull's neck and reared back hard, hauling on the leather. The car jerked and swerved as he pulled Bull farther and farther back. Bull took his hands off the wheel and clawed at his neck as he struggled frantically to pull the belt away. Unwittingly he pressed the accelerator as he fought. The car swerved wildly, then lurched over a steep embankment and slid toward the creek below.

Twitch jerked awake and struggled to get his wits about him as he realized what was happening. The force of the lunging car as it began to roll tossed him to one side. The Glock slid onto the floor and under the seat. He scrambled to retrieve it.

The Chameleon braced himself as the car nosedived off the road, narrowly missing an oncoming Coors delivery truck. There was the sound of twisting metal and shattering glass as the car tumbled end over end toward the water. Twitch was ejected by the momentum, coming to rest against a boulder. His body and neck were twisted. He died instantly.

The Chameleon's seat belt locked, pinning him against the back of the seat, but he didn't release his hold on the belt. Bull flew into the back seat, half smothering his passenger. The car came to rest upside-down in the creek.

Dazed, the Chameleon pushed Bull's body off of himself and crawled out the mangled back window, cutting his hands on jagged shards protruding from the rim. As he sprawled on the creek bank, he muttered, "Seat belts save lives." Then everything went black.

The Chameleon awakened to the distinct smell of disinfectant and the hum of an air conditioning unit sputtering in an unsynchronized cadence.

"What the . . . who are you?" the Chameleon asked the startled CNA.

"I'm . . . Heidi Fields . . . I'm . . ." She did not finish her sentence or the bed bath and hastily gathered up the basin and washcloth and started for the door. Realizing she had left the towel on the bed, she retreated and the two reached for the towel at the same time. The Chameleon won the tug-of-war and immediately covered himself.

The door swung open and a burly man in

a rumpled button-down shirt entered the room. "Is everything all right?" he asked as the CNA squeezed past him. Squinting at the Chameleon, he exclaimed, "My God, you're awake. About time."

The Chameleon could see his reflection in the mirror across the room. His head and parts of his upper body were covered in bandages. "I hope I'm not paying by the square inch," he muttered as he tried to stifle the throbbing he felt throughout his six-foot-five frame. "Where the hell am I, and what day is this?"

The man, a police officer, was already on his radio reporting the news that the patient was conscious. "Um . . . Yes, sir . . . Of course, sir . . . See you in ten." The man then returned the radio to the leather case strapped to his belt. "Sorry about that," he said to the Chameleon.

"I know I'm in a hospital . . . but which one? And, who are you?" The Chameleon was trying to make sense of it all and could now feel the stinging sensation on the outside of his windpipe. When he touched it, he winced in pain.

"I wouldn't do that if I were you, warned the barrel shaped man, frowning. "My name is

13

The CHAMELEON

Bert Cavanah. I'm a detective with the Denver Police Department and assigned by Chief Seaton to guard you on a rotation basis along with officers Floyd Burrows and Homer Parker. You're at St. Luke's Hospital in Denver and are under police protection."

The Chameleon grimaced and rubbed his forehead. "The last thing I remember was being in a car that ran over a steep embankment in Clear Creek Canyon. My seatbelt jammed and…."

"That was ten days ago," Bert said. "The only thing I know is that you've been in a comma since you were admitted, and only your doctor and medical staff are allowed into your room. Even housekeeping must work in the presence of authorized personnel."

"What happened to the two characters I was riding with?" The Chameleon groaned and struggled to pull himself into a sitting position.

"Both were pronounced dead at the scene. The media outlets reported the third occupant, namely you, as being in critical condition and not expected to live. Upon orders from the chief, no word as to your condition can be released without his knowledge and consent."

Just then, Dr. Felix Hernandez strode

into the room dutifully followed by the RN. He was a handsome, middle-aged man with olive skin and thick, black hair. A few rebellious strands fell over his forehead that made him appear more boyish and attractive. He had a no nonsense manner about him.

"You must leave now!" Dr. Hernandez barked.

"I was just going," Bert said putting up his hands in mock surrender.

You can tell who's in charge here, The Chameleon noted as he grimaced in pain.

Dr. Hernandez picked up the chart at the foot of the bed and studied it for a moment then consulted with the nurse. He walked over to the bed and began a cursory examination. The Chameleon groaned and swore as the doctor pressed on his bruised ribs. Hernandez stood up and adjusted the stethoscope hanging around his neck and jammed his hands into the pockets of his white coat. "You are a lucky man," he told the Chameleon. "I'm Dr. Hernandez and you have been under my care. Nice to see you awake. Even though you will have a lot of pain, your prognosis is good. Do you remember anything about the accident?"

The Chameleon shrugged and shook his head.

"You crawled out of the vehicle, but your seatbelt very likely saved your life. Your pelvis and ribs are badly bruised, your right shoulder was dislocated, and you suffered a concussion. Like I said, you'll have some pain but the fact that you are alive is as close to being a miracle as I've seen in awhile."

The Chameleon opined that Dr. Hernandez would be taking credit for having raised his patient from the dead.

Hernandez smiled and brushed absently at the unruly hair over his forehead. He ordered a morphine drip and left the room. The IV had barely been set up when Chief Russell Seaton entered his hospital room. As the door swung open, the Chameleon could see the number on the door: 1111. "A lucky hand," he said to himself, "four aces."

"Why are you looking at me like that?" the Chameleon managed to ask suddenly feeling the warm sensation of the morphine as it coursed through his system.

"I was worried about you, Chris," Chief

Seaton replied as he clamped an affectionate hand on the Chameleon's shoulder. "It's only a matter of time before a press release is issued officially announcing the death of Vincenti Bari Mazzini, also known in the undercover sting as Vinnie. It will announce your death as well."

"Chief, tell me," the Chameleon asked as the morphine began to ease the pain and dull his brain, "will the release give my alias or my legal name Christopher Claudio Carcelli?"

"Good question, Chris. I assume your family, as well as the Chicago Police Department, would want to use your real name. Even though you are on loan to us, you would still have been considered as having been killed in the line of duty."

"Now why are you looking at *me* funny?" Chief Seaton asked.

"If you only knew…" The Chameleon held a secret that neither Chief Seaton, nor the CPD knew about. The Chameleon had been christened Donato Leonardo Mira, Jr. and his name had been changed as part of a witness protection program many years before.

"If Marcus Sagibaro and his powerful

crime family believe you died along with his two henchmen, they will be lulled into a false sense of security and provide the nails for their own coffins. We needn't be in a hurry to prosecute them. 'Give them enough rope and they hang themselves' as we say in the trade."

"How do we stage my death?"

"Upon your release, we actually transport you to the morgue. At the morgue, you are escorted away and we use the body of a John Doe and substitute the John Doe for Vincenti Bari Mazzini."

"Say what?"

"I know, it sounds extreme actually hauling you to the morgue, but I assure you, Sagibaro will be watching our every move. With a body in a coffin and a formal ceremony at the cemetery, no one will be the wiser. Between that and the attendant publicity, all will be aware—and more importantly *convinced*—of Vincenti Bari Mazzini's death."

"So you provide me with a disguise and I return to my job at the CPD with only a few 'scratches' to chronicle my ordeal?"

"And, we continue to infiltrate the Sagiboro drug family by more subtle methods.

Before Chief Seaton left, the Chameleon succeeded in convincing him that it would be ill-advised for the Chameleon to release his true name or stage his own death. As far as the world knew, the deceased was not an undercover operative but a hood named Vincenti Bari Mazzini

On the last day of September 2006, at the age of forty-eight, Vincenti Bari Mazzini was laid to rest at a private but publicized ceremony at Our Lady of Lourdes Cemetery in Golden, Colorado. "May his soul rest in peace," those few assembled were heard to pray as Vincenti Bari Mazzini ceased to be—or so it appeared.

CHAPTER ONE

1980

When Christopher Claudio Carcelli started with the Chicago Police Department as a patrolman, he had just graduated from the University of Chicago where he was a criminal justice/police science major. He was still wet behind the ears and had barely graduated from the academy when his value as a law enforcement officer would be determined and ultimately define his career.

Chris, as he was then called, was assigned to walk the beat along what was referred to as the Magnificent Mile in downtown Chicago. Upon hearing an alarm during his first week of duty, he darted to its source and discovered a robbery in progress at a well known jewelry store. As the lone robber brandishing a .357 Smith & Wesson revolver exited the establishment, he was accosted by Chris, who by then had drawn his service revolver. The robber disregarded Chris' command to drop the weapon and put his hands in the air and instead fired his weapon in Chris' direction, grazing Chris' left shoulder. Chris' aim was more accurate as he fired before the robber could squeeze off a second shot. The county medical examiner listed the robber's cause of death as "rupture of the heart."

The following week, while doing a security check on the rear entrance of several businesses, Chris discovered three hoodlums in the alley pummeling what later turned out to be a DEA undercover officer. Chris not only subdued and arrested the ruffians, but succeeded in eliciting information from one of the three that resulted in a sizable drug bust. Chris was soon earning the admiration and respect of his fellow officers and attracting the attention of his superiors. He was promoted to the detective corps and used in some extra-sensitive undercover operations. He had his father's investigative instincts and the guts of a burglar. He was smart and had the capacity to get out of dangerous situations. His peers called him a real life superhero, impervious to harm–invincible.

The CHAMELEON

He was young and cocky, and seemed to be on a mission. He volunteered for the most dangerous assignments.

By the time Chris was twenty-eight and had been with the CPD a half dozen years, he had been involved in some well-publicized sting operations involving some prominent crime figures and corrupt politicians. As an undercover officer, he had been cast in a variety of roles, some of which required extensive research to pull them off. He had convincingly played the part of a drug dealer, druggie, pharmacist, professional photographer, film director, journalist, pimp, radio show host, television producer, business executive, insurance salesman, stock broker, psychologist, physician and a lawyer.

Not only was Chris required to act the part but to look the part as well. He soon became the master of disguise in addition to being the master of deception. He had the uncanny knack of gaining and losing weight. He was adept at growing a ponytail and shaving his head and everything in between. He changed the color of his hair so often that only his hairdresser knew for sure. He tailored the facial hair and color to suit the occasion, and kept the costume department at the CPD busy designing the appropriate wardrobe. Because of the physical change in body shape and size, the CPD always had a tailor on stand-by and Chris soon became The Great Imposter.

Chris had to be unpredictable to go undetected. He could compromise his cover by just testifying in court, since hearings and trials were usually open to the public. In high-profile cases, his photograph going to and coming from court would oftentimes be prominently displayed on the front page of the newspaper or the television screen, lending to his potential exposure. There were only so many disguises he could conjure up that would ensure his anonymity. Going undetected was the key ingredient in obtaining incriminatory evidence and convictions, maintaining job security, and more importantly, in preserving his life.

If there was anything that would betray him, it was the St. Christopher medal he wore on a chain around his neck. It had been his father's and was given to him by his mother the day he graduated from the police academy. He referred to it as his "sacred talisman" and he never took it off.

The CHAMELEON

He credited it with having carried him through some vexing and perilous situations.

Every time he embarked on a caper, he first made sure he was wearing his St. Christopher medal and, fingering it, would usually utter a short prayer or two. He would then be reminded of what his father would customarily say before embarking upon a particularly dangerous assignment: *There is no fudge factor when you are playing a high-stakes game with hardened criminals. They are skeptical to begin with and are themselves, masters of deceit. It is not easy to out-con a con. If you do, and live to tell about it, you deserve an Oscar.*

His father, unfortunately, was not there to talk about it. Chris remembered the day he thought he would meet the same fate. It was in late autumn and he had gone undercover posing as a wholesaler in a meth manufacturing operation in Chicago's famous South Side. A police informant had provided information, but not enough to obtain an arrest warrant or even a search warrant for that matter. It was Chris' assignment to obtain the ammo or probable cause necessary to effectuate the bust.

After laying the ground work necessary to gain the confidence of a worker bee, Chris was taken to the beehive and soon integrated into the circle of intimates. When the head of operations became suspicious of Chris' loyalty, or maybe a test of Chris' fortitude, he stuck a .38 Smith & Wesson to Chris' left temple. He slowly pulled back the hammer and put his finger on the trigger. He sneered that he suspected Chris to be a police informant and that his organization had a no-tolerance policy for snitches. Chris felt his body reacting as his heart began to race. With a sheer act of will, he stood motionless, concentrating to regulate his breathing and heart rate. Chris neither said nor did anything to suggest complicity.

The man pulled the trigger as the hammer came down with a click. He threw back his head and laughed as he shoved Chris aside. Chris's knees threatened to buckle, but he refused to let them. He neither flinched nor otherwise reacted. When it was over, he had passed the screening process and was unconditionally accepted into the fold. Later, Chris' infiltration into this group became the ultimate bust, garnering over a dozen convictions. From that moment on, Chris was dubbed by his fellow detectives as The

The CHAMELEON

Chameleon—a man with a thousand faces and nerves of steel.

CHAPTER TWO

1987

At the Chameleon's twenty-ninth birthday party, held at the home of a fellow detective, Rolland Harken, he was introduced to Rolland's twenty-five-year-old sister, Sandy. She was a beautiful woman, smart, educated, tall and athletic, with long tawny hair. Just plain gorgeous was how the Chameleon described her to his mother. The Chameleon was smitten with her blue-green eyes, olive complexion and perfect smile.

Eight days before Christmas, six months from the day they were introduced, Sandy became Mrs. Christopher Claudio Carcelli. The wedding was held in Sandy's hometown of Cincinnati at one of the largest Catholic churches there. The Cincinnati reception was held at a country club close to her family estate. The Chicago reception was later held at the home of Sandy's brother.

Sandy was a third-generation attorney at the prestigious law firm of Harken, Morford, Lennox and Cartwright. With offices in Chicago as well as Cincinnati, Sandy's integration into the HML&C branch in Chicago was but a mere formality. There she would work until the middle of the second trimester while pregnant with their oldest daughter, Caitlin. Within eighteen months after the birth of Caitlin, their second daughter, Chelsea, was born.

Sandy worked hard at being a mom and wife and spent less time working at the firm. The Chameleon was obsessed with his police work and was unabashed in declaring it came first, right or wrong. Sandy had theorized that it was the yearning to solve his father's murder and bringing the perpetrator or perpetrators to justice that propelled him. She had given him ultimatums during their years together, and finally in desperation had thrown in the towel. Even with a beautiful family, a nice home and successful careers, Chris and Sandy divorced in 2002. Caitlin was thirteen and Chelsea eleven. After the divorce, Sandy moved back to Cincinnati with the girls, and went back to work full-time in the home office of her father's law firm.

The Chameleon admitted that his occupation and preoccupation had made life less than desirable for Sandy and the girls. It was the nature of the beast. There was no such thing as a part-time undercover-cop, and no way to effectively serve two masters. Putting his family on the back burner was a realization he did not particularly relish. He initially felt it was temporary. That allowed him to rationalize away the guilt. However, it was not only his wife and daughters who were affected. His mother, now in her seventies, had pleaded with him to spend more time with his family and "not be like your father." The Chameleon had even become somewhat estranged from his brothers. His career was his whole life and its exclusivity had shut out everyone and everything. For that, he would not be the only one who would pay a heavy price.

The CHAMELEON

In his mind, his job was more than just playing cops and robbers. Catching the perpetrator in the act was oftentimes the least complex and least problematic. There were constraints imposed by the federal and state constitutions, not to mention the various legislations with which he had to contend. The judicial branch presented its own brand of challenges. Because of the disparity among jurisdictions, the disparity among the judges in the same jurisdiction, and the inconsistency in the rulings of the same judges, the law was not as predictable and precise as he had first been led to believe. It was as elusive as trying to retrieve a straw hat in a swirling wind.

Particularly perplexing was the range and the caliber of prosecuting attorneys and the cheapshot artists he and his department commonly referred to as defense attorneys. The key defense to all undercover busts was entrapment. It was asserted regardless of the circumstances. Once raised by even a scintilla of evidence, it was incumbent upon the prosecution to disprove it. Under the defense, if an accused was induced to commit a crime by a law enforcement officer and wouldn't have done so except for the inducement, his or her act would not be considered criminal. On the other hand, if the law enforcement officer merely afforded the accused an opportunity to commit a crime for which he or she was predisposed to commit, that was not considered entrapment. The latter would be considered legitimate detection and efficient and resourceful eradication of crime and criminals. The problem, however, was how to tell the difference.

Even if the trial judge ruled in the prosecution's favor, there was always the chance that some appellate court would overturn the conviction—usually on some technicality. Cases could languish for years as criminal cases coursed their way through the appellate process, sometimes traveling as far as the United States Supreme Court. If the conviction was reversed, the case would usually be re-tried and everyone would be back at ground zero proceeding through the court mire as if for the very first time. Finality was a distant dream and, in the interim, such cases would be filed away in the archives of the mind in the category of "unfinished business." It was one of the worrisome aspects of the Chameleon's business. Most was beyond his control, but not all.

CHAPTER THREE

────────────

2007

The wind off Lake Michigan provided some natural air-conditioning on what ordinarily would have been a stifling July day. With only two days before Independence Day and three days before his mother's seventy-third birthday, the Chameleon was experiencing anxiety over an appropriate gift for his mother. She always protested his buying anything since she always said she had more than she needed and couldn't get rid of what she had. He knew, however, she would be disappointed with just a card.

As he strode down Michigan Avenue north of the main downtown area and along his old beat, the Magnificent Mile, he browsed through many of the elegant shops on both sides of the street, finding only disappointment.

About to declare defeat, he spied a turquoise pant suit displayed in the window of an upscale shop. It was his mom's favorite color and a perfectly suited style for her age. The suit was complemented with a nicely tailored white blouse. Perfect. If he didn't get this right, he knew it would end up at Goodwill as had happened in the past. The silk robe he gave her for Christmas mysteriously disappeared, and was described in a letter to Sandy and her granddaughters as frivolous and scanty.

He had passed Magnelli's Boutique many times in the past and did little more than stick his head in the door on several occasions. He hated to shop and only went through the motions to placate Sandy and when his job required it. He was surprised as he entered Magnelli's Boutique at the pleasant smell and variety of exquisite ladies' apparel. The shop was busier than he had expected and he was impressed by the stylish clerks. One of them was a woman he presumed to be in her late thirties or early forties with long, black, flowing hair. She wore a navy blue dress with white collar and cuffs, and a hemline adequately displaying her shapely legs. She was busy arranging merchandise when he walked in. He stood there for a moment then cleared his throat in a lame attempt to get her attention.

"Excuse me," the Chameleon finally said, thinking the better of the contemplated tap on the shoulder.

"Yes?" she inquired as though startled and somewhat perturbed.

Peering into the dark, penetrating eyes that dominated a delicate and exquisite face, the Chameleon was caught off guard. Her tone was almost scolding and she reminded him of his second-grade school teacher whose look was all that was needed to convey disapproval. Suddenly, he felt timid and insecure and he heard himself mumble and stutter something that sounded vaguely like an apology.

When her eyes softened and she managed a contrite smile, he felt like a school boy again waiting on the street corner to catch a glimpse of the pretty first grade girl at the usual spot at the usual time as she walked home from school with her friends. Just her fleeting glance would make his wait worthwhile.

"Do you have that effect on all your customers?" the Chameleon managed to ask forcing confidence.

"Only on the tall, dark and handsome ones," she responded. "Welcome to Magnelli's. Is this your first time in our boutique?"

"Actually, this my first time in the boutique as a live, or should I say, paying customer. I've been in here a few times in the past when I was patrolling the Magnificent Mile as a street cop. I'm trying to purchase a birthday gift for a mother who is difficult to shop for. She will be seventy-three on the fifth and, in the past, has not exactly been delighted by what she considered my ill-conceived gift selections."

"July fifth? That's my father's birthday, only he will be eighty-three," she said, smiling. "I have just unpacked some very stylish dresses that would be age appropriate for your mother." With this she directed her attention to the rack with which she had been previously preoccupied. "Do you know her size?"

"Seven. No, I'm sorry, that was my ex-wife's size. My mother wears a size six." The

The CHAMELEON

Chameleon hoped the Freudian slip wouldn't be interpreted as a deliberate revelation of availability.

With no apparent reaction to the innuendo, she stated, "That elegant turquoise pant suit on display in the front window is a size six. The white blouse, which is priced separately, would be a perfect fit as well."

"I know you're not going to believe this, but that's what attracted my attention to begin with. That's the reason I came into your boutique. Hopefully, I will not have to wash windows and clean floors to pay for it."

"If you purchase the pant suit and the blouse, I'll knock off fifty dollars. With the discount, that would come to around three hundred forty-five dollars for the two."

"With that, you should throw in the manikin and the shoes. Do you think your boss would approve?"

"I *am* the boss," she said emphatically. "And, if the shoes will fit your mother, they're yours. Fair deal?"

The Chameleon's timidity had not completely dissipated and he was of the frame of mind that he would buy anything she had to sell. He was taken aback by her beauty, elegance and charm and he was already scheming as to how he might arrange for a private showing. When she asked if he wanted the items gift wrapped, he availed himself of the opportunity mainly to get up the nerve to make a play.

While she waited on him, the Chameleon observed no wedding band or engagement ring. He assumed she was available but was fearful she already had unyielding commitments. Furthermore, a rejection would be just as disastrous and perhaps more devastating than his pride would allow. He wasn't sure he wanted to take the chance. Besides, was this woman completely out of his league?

When she completed the sale and handed back his credit card, she said, "Thank you Christopher C. Carcelli."

Seizing upon the opportunity, the Chameleon asked for her name. She said, "Meloni Magnelli but the name on my birth certificate is Melonaya Angelina Baranetti. Because my shops carry my ex-husband's name, I still go by his name. My friends, however, just call me Meloni. You may call me that if you wish."

The CHAMELEON

The Chameleon's heart was racing and he was scolding himself for his cowardice. Facing the baddest of the bad and having to avoid life threatening mistakes was one thing, but walking this tightrope was something for which he was totally unprepared. He could not identify, let alone assume the character, for just such occasion. His systems just seemed to shut down and in her engaging stare, he felt exposed, insecure and, worst of all, vulnerable.

Meloni smiled at his discomfiture. "I didn't have breakfast. I'm going to Desolina's and grab an early lunch. Would you care to join me? My treat. Part of the promo package, along with the shoes." She laughed pleasantly.

The Chameleon returned her smile. "If I'd known I'd get a date with you, I wouldn't have quibbled over the price." He held out his arm, and she put hers through his.

The delicatessen was little more than a hole in the wall. Most of the interior was taken up by a display case filled with meats, cheeses, and other food, a selection that apparently was meant to appeal to a wide variety of ethnic groups.

The man behind the counter called, "Hey, Meloni. What you havin' today?"

"Hi, Al. I'll have a hot pastrami on pumpernickel and a side of German potato salad." She turned to Chris, her eyebrows raised.

"Double that," he said to Al. "And a large limeade. Make that two," he added when Meloni nodded.

In less than three minutes, they were carrying their plates to one of the small wrought iron tables that would have been more at home in an old-fashioned soda shop. Chris set down his plate and pulled out a chair for Meloni. She settled gracefully onto the seat and spread a napkin across her lap. He sat and took a bite of potato salad.

She sipped her drink then held the chilled glass to the side of her neck. "I wouldn't be surprised if we set a record for heat today."

"Hottest July I can remember," Chris said, biting into the crisp kosher dill that accompanied his sandwich.

After they'd eaten, Meloni took a business card from her purse. "Let me know if the clothes don't fit."

The Chameleon took the card and handed her one of his. "I'm usually a size 46 extra long."

The CHAMELEON

Meloni gave him a puzzled look, then started to chuckle.

"I take it you were not referring to my clothes," the Chameleon said with a grin.

"Your clothing is the least of your problems," Meloni said as she raised her glass in a toast, and Chris tapped it with his, not yet knowing they would soon be engulfed in events that most people found only between the pages of a novel.

CHAPTER FOUR

O n the eve of Independence Day, the Chameleon was surprised to find a voice message from Meloni when he arrived at his three-room, garden-level apartment in Edison Park that evening. "Thanks for humoring me with the early lunch. Sorry for the rush and lack of privacy. Wondered if you would be my guest tomorrow afternoon at my cousin's annual Fourth of July extravaganza. Call me on my cell phone if you are interested."

The Chameleon experienced an inexplicable adrenaline rush. After their chance encounter and brief moment together, the Chameleon had written Meloni off as an impossible dream, an unrealistic expectation, and what he had come to consider a past happening.

41

The CHAMELEON

The Chameleon had calculated his life would go on uninterrupted without her. Now, suddenly, there was a resurgence of purpose and anticipation. He had been obsessing about the reasons he had not made a good first impression. He had allowed his emotions to interfere with common sense. His only mistake was thinking he made a mistake. He had not struck out after all! He was *still* at bat!

The Chameleon tapped the menu on his phone so he could get Meloni's phone number off his caller ID.

Suddenly the phone rang, and Meloni's number popped up. His pulse instantly began to race as he picked up.

Meloni's saucy greeting sounded like music to his ears. "Hello?"

"Triple C at your service, ma'am," he said.

She chuckled. "Does that mean you've accepted my invitation?"

"How could I resist? However, I will have to rearrange my social calendar to accommodate yours, which means I will have to cancel scores of appearances at various singles' bars, thus causing mass heartbreak to untold millions."

"I hope you don't think me brash, but when you refused to allow me to buy lunch, I just had to find a way to reciprocate."

"Hmm. And here I was thinking you were calling out of desire to see me again. Now, I find you are calling only out of a sense of duty. That rankles my sensitivities, not to mention my self-esteem."

"You haven't advised me of my Miranda rights, Officer" Meloni said playfully. "Can I plead the Fifth? Or, maybe you're not expecting a response, especially one that might be incriminatory in nature."

"It sounds like you should confer with an attorney," the Chameleon replied. "If you can't afford one, we can arrange to have one appointed for you."

"I'd rather meet you at Fiore di Campo Ristorante."

"Out on Northwest Highway?"

"That's the one. You can leave your car there and I'll chauffeur you to Cousin Sal's."

"Can't wait." He hung up feeling like he just hit the lottery.

The CHAMELEON

The Chameleon had trouble positioning his long legs and adjusting the seat in Meloni's late-model sea-blue Mercedes Benz 380SL.

"Here, let me help you," Meloni said somewhat impatiently as she located the fastening end and she helped him adjust the seat and the seatbelt.

When he exaggerated his confinement by scrunching down in the soft leather seat, she did not seem at all amused. "By assuming a fetal position," she said, "you not only embarrass yourself but me and the manufacturer as well. If you're trying to attract attention, you're doing a great job."

The Chameleon couldn't tell whether her deep, liquid eyes contained pity or disgust as she scolded him for being uncooperative. He rather enjoyed the coddling and her warm touch.

"I'm sorry for not having a kid seat in your size," she said sarcastically as she straightened the seat belt across his lap.

When Chris smiled at Meloni in childish delight, Meloni just shook her head.

As they drove towards Park Ridge, the Chameleon learned for the first time that Meloni's cousin was Salvatore Antonello, *the* Salvatore Antonello. Sal, as he was referred to, was well known in the legal community for his representation of mob figures both known and suspected. If Sal represented you, you were thereafter classified as a member of the underworld. It was a dead giveaway. Although Sal's methods of obtaining acquittals for his clients were somewhat questionable, his trial abilities were not. A graduate of Yale Law School, he was a polished professional with a persuasive tongue that transformed a courtroom into his personal stage. The Chameleon had felt the sting of Sal's cross-examination on more than one occasion. He couldn't help but wonder how Sal would interpret this unexpected visit as they followed the long driveway leading into the Antonello estate.

Sal was an imposing figure, tall and muscular with a handshake that left a lasting impression. Sal seemed surprised but pleased when the butler ushered Meloni and the Chameleon inside. It was immediately obvious to Meloni that the two men knew each other and had a great deal of respect for one another. Soon, the three were joined and greeted by Sal's wife of some twenty years, and obviously some twenty years younger. If it were not for her poise and grace, the Chameleon might have mistaken her for Sal's daughter. Tall, blonde and suntanned, it was apparent she was used to being pampered. Her pale, blue-grey eyes with thick lashes were striking, and her perfect white teeth framed by sensuous, glossy pink lips, only needed white wings to complete the angelic image.

"I'm Lenna," she said to the Chameleon as she extended her hand, the one containing the smaller of the two diamonds she was wearing. Not as large as the engagement ring on her left hand, which was the size of an ice cube; the one on the right hand was almost as impressive. However, it was not the rings that commanded the Chameleon's attention.

"I want to introduce my friend, Chris Carcelli, who works for the Chicago Police Department," Meloni said.

Lenna continued to hold the Chameleon's hand and looked into his eyes, pouting devilishly. "I hope you're not here on official business."

With that, everyone chortled. The Chameleon took a bag that Meloni had been holding and gave it to Lenna. She peered inside. "Ooh! Frascati and Brunello. Red and white wine. You've taken care of any eventuality. All we need now is something blue."

"I'm here on a mission of peace and this is our peace offering. At least on Independence Day, Chris for the prosecution and Sal for the defense can have a symbiotic relationship and live in harmony."

"Thanks," Lenna said.

Sal chimed in. "We can celebrate Independence Day and Armistice Day at the same time." No enemies here, it appeared, at least for this day.

As Meloni and the Chameleon were led through Park Ridge's Xanadu, the Chameleon was reminded of something his father had told him when he started grade school. "Study hard and pick an occupation or profession with a high reward-to-work ratio. If you don't want to be a medical doctor, at least consider being a defense lawyer." Now he knew what his father had meant. The Antonello family appeared to want for nothing.

The pool was elegant and almost resort-sized, in keeping with what he had just witnessed inside. And, it was obvious Sal had not spared any expense for this Fourth of July celebration. Described in her telephone message as an "extravaganza," Meloni had not been exaggerating. The Chameleon was guessing there were close to forty guests already poolside. His selection of some new casual wear for the party had been mainly for Meloni's sake. But now, he was pleased with himself for having had the foresight to have discarded his usual grubby garb. Now, he would not feel out of place hobnobbing with the rich and the famous.

When Meloni emerged from the pool house, he almost dropped his glass of Valpolicello. He had to do a double-take to make sure the beauty he was seeing was really her. She looked stunning in her marine-blue bikini and exotic sunglasses. With her hair up and her voluptuous figure–a figure that up to now had been pretty much hidden from view, the image of Lenna's bronze skin, ample breasts and sumptuous lips faded into oblivion. *Meloni is the only woman a man could ever want*, the Chameleon thought, wondering if that was really Meloni or if his eyes were just playing tricks.

"You look like you just saw a ghost," Meloni commented. "Are you okay?"

The Chameleon masked his reactions little when it came to Meloni. Meloni was a vision beyond even his most unbridled imagination. He was uncharacteristically at a loss for words. Fortunately, the two were interrupted by a pretty young server with a tray of hors d'oeuvres.

"Do I need to worry about you hustling all those shapely, thin, young things, especially the tantalizing Camille and Mindy who are glued to Sal's twin sons, Rocco and Ricco?"

"Oh, to be twenty-five again," the Chameleon quipped. "Neither Camille's nor Mindy's eyes are trained to even recognize or acknowledge the existence of someone approaching the half-century mark. I'm not even a blip on their radar screens. Besides, I'm preoccupied with admiring the beautiful guest claiming to be Sal's cousin."

The CHAMELEON

"Have you had too much Trebbiano D'Abruzzo or Valpolicello to drink, or are you merely visually impaired? Surely I can't be the only one on *your* radar screen?"

"If I were taking my annual physical right now, I would be hospitalized because of my irregular heartbeat. Here, feel for my pulse," the Chameleon said offering the wrist.

As she came close, he could smell her sweet fragrance, which caused his heart to flutter with even more fervor. As she searched for his pulse with her soft, gentle touch, he impulsively pulled her close and felt the softness and warmth of her breasts pressing against his chest and her moist, generous lips press against his. He envisioned a time when they would be alone together.

"Hey, none of that," they heard Lenna tease as she brought a bottle of Vernaccia San Gimignano to fill their glasses. "I don't want my stepsons and their dates to get the wrong impression. It is way too early for the fireworks to start."

Turning to the Chameleon, Lenna said, "Chris, Sal tells me you're responsible for some of his biggest legal fees and also responsible for most of the tarnishes on his win-loss record. With a name like Carcelli, he says, you are clearly on the wrong side of the equation."

"Like your husband, I boast of being on the right side—the side of justice. What could be more patriotic than that? Only in America could we celebrate a country's independence as 'blood brothers' one day and still align ourselves on opposite sides in the courtroom the next."

"I take it you're Italian," Lenna said sizing up the Chameleon.

"Wouldn't it be great if everyone was?" the Chameleon quipped. "By the way, what I said was not meant as a slam. Your ancestors obviously came from a different part of the globe than mine."

"My maiden name was Thibert. My father was French and my mother Norwegian. My mother had some Swedish ancestors and I have been accused of being a hybrid. Sal is Italian, as you might have guessed. However, some of his forefathers were from Italy and some reputedly from Sicily. Sometimes he claims to be Italian and other times Sicilian. If I had been able to have children, God only knows what the mix would have produced."

Although he wanted to say *Mafia popes*, the Chameleon instead responded, "Beautiful, intelligent and blessed children, I would venture to say."

"Those are my sentiments exactly," Meloni said while wrapping a free arm around the Chameleon's waist and edging closer.

Lenna set the wine on a nearby table and hugged them both. "I'm glad the two of you could make it." Turning to Meloni, Lenna said, "You two make an awesome couple. If I were you, I'd never leave home without him."

The Chameleon thought, *If Meloni and I were a couple, I'd never want to leave home! Period!* The Chameleon set his glass aside. "Race you to the shallow end," he said, grabbing Meloni's hand and tugging her toward the pool.

"You're on!" With no warning she dived in and began stroking toward the other end.

The Chameleon was hard put to keep up with her, but he managed to reach the side of the pool one stroke ahead of her. "You're really good."

"Thanks, I get lots of practice. Sal lets me use the pool whenever I want to and my folks have one at their home and several at their casino."

"I can see you enjoy the sun. That's quite a tan you have."

"Just my natural coloring from my Hawaiian ancestors. I don't even have a tan line."

The Chameleon reached toward her bikini strap.

She grinned and slapped his hand away. "Don't even think about it." But her eyes told him that there would be a time when he could verify her claim.

Noticing the Chameleon's St. Christopher medal, Meloni touched it. "Do you always wear this?"

"I never leave home without it. It belonged to my father."

Running her fingers across the medallion, she noticed the scar that marred the Chameleon's throat. "What happened?"

"Just one of the hazards of being a cop."

Meloni raised an eyebrow. "And?"

The CHAMELEON

"A long and boring story. To tell you about it now would only spoil the moment."

Their conversation was interrupted when Rocco tossed a volleyball into the water shouting, "Who's up for a game?" He plunged in splashing water on Meloni and the Chameleon. The Chameleon and Meloni ended up on the same side. For the next hour, the Chameleon felt as if he had died and gone to heaven as Meloni leapt and swung at the ball, sometimes bumping against him. He was sure she wasn't just being clumsy.

"Are you enjoying yourself, Superman?" Meloni asked in a saucy voice as she edged her body close.

"I thought you told me not to think about it," the Chameleon said feigning rejection.

"That was hours ago," Meloni taunted. "Isn't it a woman's prerogative to change her mind?"

"In this instance, yes. And I am indeed enjoying myself. In fact, I'm having a great, no make that a fantastic time."

"You're not worried about your next assignment, are you? You seem preoccupied."

"You know I'm always focused. Only this time, it is not on my next assignment but on the task at hand."

This time, it was Meloni who raised her eyebrows. "I think it's time for lunch."

Although their host had the usual Independence Day menu, including hamburgers, hotdogs, potato salad and watermelon for the children, the two sampled the Chicken Milano, baked cheese tortellini, jambalaya fettuccini, and cheese tortellini with shrimp smothered in rosemary-chipotle sauce. Later, the two would indulge in Sal's favorite dish prepared especially for him by Lenna, a recipe Sal's mother, Marriana, had given to her: baked lasagna with mozzarella cheese and pomodoro sauce.

When they had eaten their fill, Lenna rolled a drink cart to the table. "We have Grappa, Lemoncello, Campari and Montenegro."

Meloni said, "I'll have Campari."

"Make mine Lemoncello," the Chameleon said.

As they settled back to enjoy their digestif he said, "That takes me back to the family reunions in upstate New York that my mom's parents hosted each year. I never tired of Italian or Mexican food." He paused and muffled a belch with his fist. "I hope you have some Tums in your purse."

"Always. I learned a long time ago to be prepared."

Chris had lost interest in watching fireworks over the years. It was nothing like when he, Sandy and their two daughters fought the traffic to and from the Navy Pier. He remembered the girls' faces as the night sky light up with a dizzying array of manmade lightning, falling stars, and fluorescent bands of color: red, orange, yellow, green, blue, violet and even silver and gold. This year he had a front row seat in the company of a beautiful woman at a spectacular private show provided by the host, Sal Antonello.

It was close to midnight by the time Meloni dropped the Chameleon off at his car. With this Fourth of July almost in the history books, a new era was emerging for Meloni and the Chameleon. He was rethinking his priorities and not anxious to have too much more time tick off the clock before revamping his life. Was it possible to make up for lost time?

CHAPTER FIVE

The Chameleon had to call and cancel his dinner date with Meloni. He was very disappointed Meloni had been unable to join his mother and himself the week before at Bernarde's Italian Restaurant in Oakbrook. Bernarde's was his mother's favorite and her choice for her seventy-third birthday celebration. Bernarde's had originally been founded by his mother's maternal uncle, a winemaker by the name of Alphonse Gaspere Bernarde.

Meloni had flown out early in the morning of the fifth to Lake Tahoe to help celebrate her father's eighty-third birthday. She had been gone a whole week and this would have been the first time they would have been together since Sal's Fourth of July extravaganza.

The Chameleon was troubled over having missed a golden opportunity to introduce Meloni to his mother and his mother to Meloni. And, unbeknownst until the last minute, both of his brothers, Francis and Anthony, flew out to be with their mother on her special day. *Meloni could have met the whole Carcelli clan in one quick swoop,* he thought. He had to admit to himself, however, that the real cause of his consternation was his inability, at least for the moment, to showcase the most captivating woman he had ever met.

The night before Meloni was due back from her parents' home at Lake Tahoe, the Chameleon called her cell phone to cancel their date.

"How long has it been since I last saw you?" Meloni asked.

"Too long," the Chameleon sighed. "As they say, absence makes the heart grow fonder."

"As they say, out of sight out of mind."

"Touché. The bad news is I'll be gone for two weeks."

"What's the good news?"

"I'll be back in two weeks!"

"Where are you off to this time?"

"The same state you're in."

"What part?"

"Can't tell you. It's a military secret."

"Couldn't be Las Vegas, could it?"

"Sorry, can't tell you until I get back."

"You always keep me in suspense!"

"Me, too!"

"Be sure to wear your medal. I want you back in one piece."

"Pray for me."

"I always do."

Even before they hung up, the Chameleon felt guilty about leaving. It was the same chapter, just a different verse in his establishment of priorities, and the predicted ebb and flow his profession had on his personal life.

The Chameleon had been involved in a number of sensitive operations in Las Vegas and was brought in as "fresh bait" from time to time. All the assignments were tangled, intricate and dangerous. So far, all had involved illegal drugs. If there was even a trace or a hint he was a narc, he would most certainly just disappear without even an indication he had ever existed. As the plane made its descent into Las Vegas, the Chameleon recounted the last time he was on assignment in Las Vegas. The two targets on that caper were not to be trifled with and had reputedly more notches on their gun stocks than Bonnie and Clyde.

Flanked by the two mobsters and another undercover cop, the Chameleon rode the up escalator in one of the casinos. Passing by on the escalator headed down he recognized a prosecutor from Chicago accompanied by his wife. As the two passed, the prosecutor smiled and said, "Hi, Chris. What are you doing here?"

The Chameleon kept his face impassive and shook his head slightly.

The prosecutor frowned, realizing his blunder. "Sorry. My mistake," he muttered.

One of the mobsters turned and gave the Chameleon a sharp look and asked, "You know that guy?"

The Chameleon remembered shrugging and saying something like, "I never saw him before. Happens all the time—one of those faces, I guess."

That was not the first time the Chameleon had been recognized by well-meaning acquaintances. Fortunately they were quick reads.

He wondered what would happen if the greeter grew suspicious and pushed the point. He figured it was like a flip of a coin. No matter how many times the coin turned up heads, it was still a fifty-fifty chance the coin would turn up heads on the next toss. He didn't want to think about the consequences in the event the coin happened to turn up tails. If it did, it would be a death warrant.

Las Vegas was a good place for undercover work. Everything was happening so quickly that there was hardly time to create error or detect it. Make-believe was the very essence of the area's existence and accounted for its continued survival. Nothing was predictable in Las Vegas, and there were no expectations. Some of the stakes were higher than others, and futures could be determined irrevocably upon one roll of the dice. Identities could be lost in the muddle; who you were didn't matter as much as what you were. Everything was measured by the almighty dollar. When they say, "What happens in Vegas stays in Vegas," they mean that what money is brought into Vegas from the far reaches of the earth, and is left on the tables, never returns to its place of origin. It is true Las Vegas was built by gamblers, but not from their winnings.

The beautiful and exquisite casinos represent heaven on earth and are thought to foretell what to expect in paradise. Clearly, owners of casinos are primary stakeholders and the intended beneficiaries of Las Vegas. Customers, even those who dissipate their life savings, would probably also be considered primary beneficiaries, albeit fitting into the class of unintended beneficiaries in most cases. Secondary stakeholders, those indirectly benefiting from the gaming operations, would no doubt be the ladies of the night and drug dealers. Las Vegas attracts all kinds. There is something for everyone, even undercover agents.

Las Vegas is not tolerant of blemishes on its reputation, and for the most part is not criminally driven. It makes a genuine effort to keep its visitors safe, secure and insulated from the undesirable. It is swiftly becoming family oriented and family friendly. Occasionally, there are those, who for one reason or another, want to change its image for the worse. And, there are those who are determined for obvious reasons not to let that happen.

The Chameleon was met by Dustin Baldwin at McCarran International Airport. Baldwin was the head of the detective bureau for the Las Vegas Police Department.

"Welcome back to Las Vegas!" Dustin greeted as he extended his right hand.

"Can't get rid of a bad penny," the Chameleon reminded him as the two shook hands and patted each other on the shoulder.

Dustin still sported a crew cut, a telltale sign of his vintage. Slim built and a half foot shorter than the Chameleon, he would never be mistaken for the Chameleon's identical twin.

"Wearing that ponytail made me wonder if that was really you," Dustin said. "And, with that beard, you look like a biker."

"Wait till you see my tattoos," the Chameleon laughed. Lifting up his black T-shirt he exposed the head of a ferocious tiger ready to strike. "Look authentic enough?"

"Doesn't wash off easily, I hope," Dustin chided. "We need to find a few more for your arms to make you believable."

"When do I get introduced to the Bartolini brothers?"

"Salvatore and Pasquale are out of the country and won't be back until the end of next week. According to our intel, they are in Columbia arranging for imports."

The Chameleon leaned closer. "Is Carlos Abetini still working undercover?"

Looking around, Dustin replied, "Not only has Abetini infiltrated the Bartolini drug ring and on the verge of identifying the kingpin for whom the Bartolini brothers are fronting, but he is accompanying Salvatore and Pasquale on their latest buying trip."

"I thought the international connection was reserved for the feds?"

"Abetini has been dating one of the sisters of the Bartolini brothers, a knockout by the name of Lucrezia. The two I think are being used as a masquerade in order to divert attention away from the brothers and thus legitimatize the purpose of the brothers' travels."

"The dossier on the brothers indicates that they are not ones to be trifled with. Messing with their sister may not be such an enviable position to be in. A fickle sister with two unsavory brothers with questionable drug connections is like playing with TNT!"

"'Tis a highly volatile situation, to be sure. However, it is something over which the LVPD has little or no control. Carlos is not someone we can afford to lose. In fact, that is why we have sent for you. Carlos needs a guardian angel, and because of the current circumstances, we have had to all but sever our direct contact with him for fear his cover will be blown. You know what that would mean."

"Bye-bye Carlos!"

"Precisely. Hopefully, you appreciate the risks of your new assignment. Personally, I would understand if you decline our invitation."

"It is no different than what I do on a daily basis for my home department. Undercover work is not for the timid. There is a reason why my life insurance premiums are so high."

Upon reaching the stationhouse, the Chameleon was briefed on the operation of the Bartolini brothers' drug business and the nature of the planned sting, code named Operation Simpatico. Shortly after their arrival, they were joined by Jacoby Tannenbaum of the Drug Enforcement Administration. With a chiseled face and fierce stare, the Chameleon was grateful the two were on the same side in the war against drugs.

"This is Chris Carcelli on loan from the Chicago Police Department," Dustin told Jacoby. "He's the one that I've told you about."

Sizing up the Chameleon, Jacoby said, "I just hope you're as good as they say you are." He shook the Chameleon's hand. The strength in his wide palm and thick fingers was enough to leave a lasting impression.

"Dustin has always been a master of the understatement," the Chameleon replied as he extracted his hand from Jacoby's grasp and attempted to mask the pain of the handshake.

66

Directing his question at Dustin, Jacoby asked, "Have you discussed with Chris the latest development with regard to the escalation of the Bartolini family operations abroad?"

"I filled him in briefly on the LVPD involvement via the Carlos Abetini connection with Lucrezia," Dustin replied. "However, that has been the extent thus far."

Turning to the Chameleon, Jacoby stated, "As you know, the DEA is the lead agency for law enforcement of the Controlled Substances Act. We share jurisdiction with the FBI and ICE. We also work closely with state agencies on domestic drug investigations. With regard to drug investigations abroad, that is the sole responsibility of the DEA."

The Chameleon quickly grasped Jacoby's message: Don't interfere with the investigations of the DEA—especially in the international sphere. The Chameleon was always troubled by the turf wars between the feds and the state authorities when it came to eradication of drug trafficking. *After all, didn't they all have the same goal?*

Jacoby did most of the talking. "Salvatore and Pasquale Bartolini are brothers who grew up on the east coast. They were recruited by a drug boss in Miami to set up a cocaine operation in Las Vegas. They seem to have an unlimited supply of cocaine and have established a cash and carry business that apparently eliminates the need for middlemen and debt collectors. Because of the amounts in which they deal, they consider themselves wholesalers and have the reputation of selling at competitive prices.

The Chameleon leaned back in his chair. "Not exactly the K-Mart blue light special, is it?"

"Meet Dom Amarelli," Carlos said as he introduced the Chameleon to Salvatore and Pasquale Bartolini.

Without rising from their chairs or acknowledging the Chameleon's extended hand, Salvatore motioned for him to sit in the seat next to him. Lucrezia, who was seated next to Pasquale, smiled at the Chameleon and nodded a greeting. Soon, Carlos occupied the seat next to Lucrezia and the two kissed. The sixth chair between Carlos and the Chameleon remained unoccupied.

"Carlos tells me you spent some time in the joint," Salvatore said to the Chameleon.

"On a trumped-up charge. I was only defending myself when the bum fell against the bumper of his parked truck. The coroner's report claimed death was caused from multiple blunt-force injuries. I only hit him once."

"I hear you have moved to Vegas from Indian Springs," Pasquale said.

"Actually, I spent time at High Desert State Prison near Indian Springs," the Chameleon responded. "I'm originally from California; was born and bred in LA."

"Should of known," Pasquale said as he examined the Chameleon's forearm that bore the words 'Los Angeles' in tattooed script.

"Understand you're looking to stay in Clark County," Salvatore interjected.

"Depends on the opportunities. I bore easy and gravitate towards the fast life. I've been down on my luck lately and need to get my Harley out of hock."

"According to Carlos, you're very enterprising and not afraid to get your hands dirty," Salvatore persisted.

The CHAMELEON

"Mr. Bartolini," the Chameleon began. "I
. . ."

"Call me Salvatore," Salvatore
interrupted.

"Salvatore, I do what has to be done and
have been known to cut corners." He studied his
fingernails.

Pasquale handed Carlos a crisp hundred
dollar bill and told him to take Lucrezia across the
street for lunch. He then summoned the maître d'
to bring three menus; they were ready for lunch.

It was obvious to the Chameleon which
brother was in charge and what respect was
demanded when he addressed Pasquale as "Mr.
Bartolini" he was not given any other option.

It was only as dessert was served that the
Bartolini brothers outlined the Chameleon's job
description. Pasquale dominated the conversation.

"You, no doubt, have heard of Lorenzo
Buonaretti," Pasquale began. "He works for the
main man. He is who Sal and I have to answer to.
If he is happy, then everyone is happy. Otherwise,
he can make life hell."

The Chameleon could see in Pasquale's
eyes a determination and commitment that would
not be compromised. He knew now was not the

time to probe into the identity of the main man. The secret, no doubt, was one that not even the Bartolini brothers knew.

As Pasquale made good use of his toothpick, he related, "We have tentacles in very high places including the LVPD. Everyone thinks Carlos works exclusively for the LVPD, but you know otherwise. We understand that the LVPD considers you an informant. Again, we know otherwise. If it weren't for Carlos, we would be putting you to the test. Since he and Lucrezia will be making Sal and me uncles in a few short months, we know he would not mislead us. Besides, I'm sure you value your life too much to be a snitch." Pasquale's grin at the Chameleon sent cold chills down the Chameleon's spine.

Managing a contrived grin of his own, the Chameleon nodded. "My loyalty has never been questioned," he assured Pasquale.

Pasquale shook the Chameleon's hand. Salvatore did the same but with less enthusiasm saying, "We are looking for someone who understands business in the county. We are also looking for someone who can eliminate shrinkage and dissuade those who might be tempted to dip into the till. We think you're the right man for the job."

Pasquale eyed the Chameleon's tattoos and bike attire. "Since you'll be our representative in dealing with certain governmental officials, you will need to get rid of the ponytail, trim the facial hair and hide the tattoos. Sal will introduce you to Ramon, our tailor, who can outfit you with a business suit or two and make you more presentable."

The Chameleon was surprised at the sophistication of the Bartolini brothers, particularly Pasquale, who looked more like a corporate executive than a drug dealer. *Looks are deceiving,* he mused. No wonder the Bartolini operation was so effective. The code name "Operation Simpatico" was an apt description. The brothers had elicited empathy, not enmity.

After almost two months of being Dom Amarelli, the Chameleon was no closer to identifying the main man than he was when he started. His inability to complete his mission was a disappointment and definitely a blow to his ego. His distress was enhanced, however, when less than a week after his return to Chicago, he was notified that Carlos Abetini's body had been found in a dumpster less than a block off the Strip. The Chameleon felt somebody up there must be looking out for him, as that could very easily have been him. Knowing that the Bartolini's had an informant in the LVPD doubled the risk. Who could he trust?

CHAPTER SIX

———————

The Chameleon's preoccupation with Meloni was causing him distress and anxiety. He had not been that way about any other woman and wondered if the distraction might have been a factor in the unsuccessful undercover operation just completed.

The lack of contact with Meloni the past four weeks had almost been more than he could bear. In the past he wrote the hiatuses off as coming with the territory. Sandy had realized that contact could jeopardize an assignment and she just grinned and bore it. He hoped Meloni would be just as understanding when he finally revealed his undercover activities. However, he wasn't sure it was worth the gamble.

"Hey, Superman, what are you doing back?" she asked as he entered her shop. "You've been AWOL and I'd almost forgotten what you

74

looked like. I will be with you as soon as I finish with Alba."

Dressed in a smart summer outfit that conformed to her fine lines, Meloni seemed even more radiant than he had remembered. After initialing a stack of order forms and scribbling her signature on a series of checks backed by an assortment of vouchers, she hustled Alba to the back office. "I should have been a doctor," she said referring to her handwriting and ostensibly the frivolous juggling of her appointments.

The Chameleon followed close behind. "You can take my pulse anytime," the Chameleon said as he replayed the scene at Sal's pool in his mind.

Inserting her arm through his and clasping his forearm with her free hand, she ushered him to the front door. "Come on," she ordered, "you can buy me a limeade."

Sitting at the same table at the deli, they sipped chilled limeade from tall frosted glasses while they gazed into each other's eyes and said little. If there were other customers in Desolina's that afternoon, Meloni and the Chameleon didn't notice them.

The CHAMELEON

The Chameleon's mother was disappointed that Meloni had not been able to attend her seventy-third birthday celebration. She was relentless in her desire to meet her son's new-found love. Feeling guilty and compelled to introduce Meloni to his mother, the Chameleon arranged for a return engagement at Bernarde's.

Chris's mother, Adriana was wearing the outfit he had given her for her birthday. It was not often she validated his purchases by wearing them. He wasn't sure if she wore the outfit to appease the gift giver or the proprietor of the shop where it was purchased. In either event, she looked most stylish and at least ten years younger than when she wore the loose fitting smock the night of her birthday. He was grateful she was not wearing it tonight.

The Chameleon had deliberately arrived early, as Meloni was to meet them at Bernarde's and he didn't want to keep her waiting. The maître d' smiled at the Chameleon and Adriana. "I am pleased to see you again. Will there be just the two of you this evening?"

"Actually, Leland, there will be three of us. The party we are waiting for, who should arrive shortly, can best be described in two words, foxy woman."

"I shall be on the lookout for such a woman," Leland said with a smile, his eyebrows doing an impish dance.

He ushered the two to Adriana's favorite corner table. Adriana, as usual, sat with her back to the wall, which was the custom when the Chameleon's father had been alive. Apparently, she felt she and her FBI husband would be safe from any ambush. Besides, that way she could keep tabs on everyone else in the room. She was not nosy, just curious. Her *curious* habit had not changed much over the years, the Chameleon mused.

The two had barely been seated and served a glass of Frascatti when Meloni arrived. The Chameleon must have given a fairly accurate description, as the maître d' escorted her unwaveringly to the proper table.

The CHAMELEON

Standing to greet Meloni, the Chameleon was captivated by the spaghetti-strapped dress and especially what was inside it. Meloni was as radiant as usual. He was embarrassed by his shyness when in her presence. Tonight was one of those times. She was always so self-assured. Although he had rehearsed the introduction in his head, he was muddled by the distraction. Without speaking he rose to greet her.

The two embraced, and after kissing the Chameleon on the cheek, Meloni extended her right hand to Adriana. "Mrs. Carcelli, I'm Meloni," she said. "I'm pleased that we are finally able to meet."

"The pleasure is all mine, my dear," Adriana replied, taking Meloni's hand for a moment. "I've been hearing a lot about the owner of Magnelli's. My son is usually prone to exaggeration. However, I can see in this case his description of you was, if anything, an understatement."

"Happy belated birthday," Meloni said as she presented Adrianna with a beautifully wrapped box bearing a Magnelli's sticker on its bow.

Adriana's eyes widened and her hand fluttered to her chest as she took the lovely box.

"Oh, my dear, you shouldn't have…" Her fingers plowed through the wrapping and she peeked inside. "Oh! It is beautiful!" she exclaimed.

"I hope I got the right size," Meloni said as the Chameleon pulled out a chair to seat her.

Adriana checked the label. "It's perfect." She held up the mauve summer dress against her frame, admiring its Aztec design.

"It will look great on you, Mrs. Carcelli," Meloni said. The Chameleon nodded his approval. Adriana reached over and gave Meloni's arm an affectionate squeeze. "Thank you so much my dear. This is just so lovely."

The Chameleon knew Adriana's approval of Meloni would not be without his mother's usual probing, or what the instructors at the police academy might have called an interrogation. Within a half hour, Adriana learned that Meloni's date of birth was October twenty-third, nineteen sixty-seven; that she was born in New York; that she was an only child; that her parents' names were Magdalena and Carleono Baranetti; that her mother was seventy-five and her father eighty-three; that her grandparents were from Italy; that she was raised Catholic; that she had received both her bachelor's and advanced degrees from the University of San Diego; that she had been divorced for approximately five years; and that she never had children.

"And what does your father do?" Adriana asked.

Meloni shrugged, "He's a businessman. He operates some merchandising businesses that my grandfather started. He used to own some pubs, too, but that was early in his career."

"That sounds interesting," Adriana said, "He must have quite a lot of money."

A thin smile touched Meloni's lips. "He likes to play the market. Commodities and stocks– that sort of thing."

"Do they live in Chicago, too?"

"No. They moved to Lake Tahoe about twenty years ago. Daddy has controlling interest in Carleono's Holiday Casino & Resort."

"What about your ex?" Adriana continued.

The Chameleon felt sweat start on his forehead. He was about to change the subject when Meloni spoke.

"He was a stockbroker. We divorced. I moved to Chicago."

Meloni asked, "So, Mrs. Carcelli, tell me about yourself."

Adriana said, "Not much to tell. We're pretty ordinary. I was widowed early and my boys have grown up just the way their father would have wanted."

The Chameleon had never told Meloni or anyone else about being part of a federal protection program and having been relocated to Chicago complete with a change in name and identity. Nor had he told her about his father having been in the FBI, having been assigned to the state of New York, and having been killed by what was thought to be members of the underworld. He had been deliberately evasive, and frankly, he had not been exposed to any of the details centered around the death of his father. His mother, even to this day, had insulated him and his brothers from knowledge that if revealed and fell into the wrong hands could still compromise the safety of the rest of the family. All he knew is that he was never to reveal his true name. No one was to ever know that he was born Donato Leonardo Mira, Jr.

The CHAMELEON

Meloni was quickly becoming the daughter Adriana always desired. Whether planning a sporting or other event or occasion in the days and weeks that followed, Meloni was quick to suggest that the Chameleon's mother be included. The Chameleon was beginning to wonder if maybe that was Meloni's way of ensuring that she remain virtuous, as demanded by her religious upbringing. He discounted the chaperon theory, however, when he observed the genuine interaction of the two women—one who he had loved since his birth and the other with whom he was falling helplessly in love.

CHAPTER SEVEN

His father's work schedule had played havoc with planned family events and had made social events a hit or miss proposition. The Chameleon remembered the sting of disappointment when his father, at the last minute, withdrew from the much anticipated trip to California and Disney Land the summer between his first and second grades. He and his brothers were heartbroken because they could not accompany their neighbors on a joint trip that had been planned for over a year.

Being an FBI agent had its benefits and its detriments. His father had said he wasn't sure he could withstand the monotony of a nine-to-five job and seemed to thrive on the spontaneous nature of his work schedule—a schedule he referred to as a misnomer and an aberration. He prided himself on his flexibility and adaptability. Yet, he preached planning, preparedness and predictability to his sons.

The Chameleon never heard his mother complain, even when the main meal of the day stood in the oven with its freshness dissipating with the setting of the sun. He was not too young to see disappointment written on her face when Sunday dinner was interrupted by an emergency call from the bureau chief and his father was whisked away on still another sensitive assignment. He also remembered numerous times when his parents, dressed and ready to enjoy an evening together, had to call the babysitter at the last minute to cancel the engagement because his father had just received another disruptive telephone call. He envied his friend whose father was a medical doctor and was on call only every fourth week. His own father was on call on a moment's notice and usually at the most inopportune time.

As he thought back, his life with Sandy and his daughters had not been much different. Fortunately, Sandy's job obligations as an attorney occurred during regular business hours and seldom did they interfere with her personal life.

With flexibility built into her schedule, she was able to fill in the gaps caused by the Chameleon's erratic schedule. However, she was not as patient and compliant as his mother. Sandy was of a different generation and tolerance was sparse in her DNA. The Chameleon marveled at how Sandy had stuck it out for over fifteen years. It was inevitable she would give him his marching papers. He tried not to allow himself time for regrets.

Meloni's business sorority was holding its fall formal dance and fashion show to raise funds for the city's underprivileged. It was a gala affair that captured the attention of the business and professional communities and was accompanied by a silent auction that in the previous year had generated in excess of one hundred thousand dollars. It was always held at one of the landmark hotels and the one-hundred-dollar-a-plate dinner was considered a bargain.

The CHAMELEON

Meloni was president of the Kappa Alpha Nu, completing the end of her two-year term. She was excited by not just having an escort this year but by having the Chameleon at her side and being able to showcase the man of her dreams. She had a daring evening gown custom made, the nature of which she had not even revealed to the Chameleon.

Selecting the tuxedo was not as traumatic as the Chameleon had expected. Meloni could not get over how handsome the Chameleon looked in a tux and the Chameleon was delighting in all the attention it generated. Playing dress-up, especially for Meloni, was not in the least bit distasteful. He was even unabashed when he modeled it for his mother.

The Chameleon was mesmerized by the elegance of the apparition, as he would later describe it, of God's handiwork that he was now holding close in his arms. He felt self-conscious and awkward as he gingerly led Meloni around the dance floor. Everything appeared surreal and if ever the Chameleon felt like an imposter, being someone he wasn't, it was now. He felt unworthy of the moment and, without question, unworthy of the woman.

It was while in this dream world that Meloni was exposed to the unpredictable nature of a career in law enforcement.

"Is that your pager?" Meloni asked as the device on the Chameleon's belt emitted its eerie tone.

"Unfortunately, yes," the Chameleon complained as he led her off the floor. "I'm sorry but I have to take this." He retrieved the message, scowling.

His mother had experienced disappointment of this nature and so had Sandy. However, it was not something he particularly wanted foisted on Meloni. Sandy had been resilient and accepting at first and then grew cynical and contemptuous. The Chameleon didn't want to squander his second chance at love.

"You look like you've just been turned into a pillar of salt," Meloni exclaimed. "Did you do something to evoke the ire of the gods?"

"Worse than that," the Chameleon replied. "In the blink of an eye my heavenly rapture, and perhaps yours, at least for the time being, has been cast into oblivion."

"Does that mean that you have been evicted from heaven and will now be cast into the fiery furnace of hell?"

"In a manner of speaking…"

"Are you telling me duty calls and that matters of significance supersede the trifling and the frivolous?"

"You are anything but trifling and frivolous. You are the alpha and everything else in this universe is the omega. However, I have no control over the inopportune caper my informant has advised me is about to unfold. Without me there, six months of infiltration and surveillance will have been for naught."

"Then by all means, don't think twice about trading ecstasy for the extraneous. Will you take me home or do I need to call for a cab?"

"I am really sorry. This is the last thing I wanted this evening–to trade a dream for a nightmare. I would understand if you chose to trade me in for a more worthwhile model. I hope you will find it within your heart to forgive me. I shouldn't be too long."

"There is nothing to forgive. I understand perfectly life's interruptions. My mother has tolerated the uncertainties all these years with my father and the interruptions have only intensified their longing and love for each other."

"Does that mean you love me?"

"Don't read between the lines, Superman. It only means that I understand the demands of life and those exerted on the special few. I will catch a ride with the Putnams in the event you are detained."

"Don't worry. I'll be back before you know it."

The Chameleon didn't know quite how to interpret Meloni's reaction, only that it was not cynical and contemptuous.

Grundel Ormandi had been a small-time hood in Chicago for at least two decades. Now in his late sixties, he had a record longer than the burning tail of a falling star. He ran a modern-day version of a speakeasy. Barry's Babes & Bar featured prostitution, drugs and gambling. Over a period of time, the two-bit operation had become a booming success. Much of what Triple B's, as it was known, attributed to its success was its unique and extensive credit arrangements. Touted by patrons for being able to put everything on the cuff, Triple Bs did a landslide business. Its strong-arm tactics in collecting past due accounts, however, was coming under the close scrutiny of law enforcement authorities, particularly the Cook County Sheriff's Office and the CPD.

Not unlike domestic abuse cases, and for some of the same reasons, the battered were anything but cooperative in fingering the true cause of their infirmity. It was amazing how many patrons of Triple Bs were admitted to the ER, ostensibly having fallen down the stairs, accidentally walked into kitchen cabinets or suffered a variety of unfortunate household "accidents". Then there were those who were deeply in debt to Triple Bs whose bodies were turning up with regularity in the far reaches of Cook County. All in all, the attrition rate among the errant patrons was becoming epidemic.

The Chameleon and several of the most adroit of the imposters in his unit, along with some from the CCSO, were conscripted to form a strike force whose goal was to cripple Ormandi's operation. The secret sting was nicknamed

Operation BINGO (the acronym for Bring In Grundel Ormandi). It would be one of the Chameleon's most dangerous assignments. If failure to pay a past due account warranted the death penalty, then what punishment would be exacted for an infiltrator, a turncoat and/or a foe, whose true identity and intention were exposed? The Chameleon's experience in the past had already provided the likely answer.

To go undercover as a Triple Bs customer and incur a sizable gambling debt would not be that difficult. The BINGO unit however, wasn't sure in what form the first notice of the past due account and demand for payment would come. None wanted to learn firsthand. The Chameleon had experienced a cracked rib or two on more than one occasion and a fractured patella while trying to subdue an irate husband in a domestic dispute. It pained him just to think about the risks. The challenge was how to catch G.O. with his hands in the cookie jar and live long enough to testify against him.

The Achilles' heel was G.O.'s thirty-five-year-old stepson, Barry Palsonde. Barry was a drug dealer and heroin addict who had been in law enforcement's cross-hairs now for quite some time. He was as elusive as an eel.

Barry was a rather imposing individual and had shoulders that made him look like he was wearing NFL shoulder pads. When he was in the eighth grade, his health records listed his height as six feet three inches and his weight at an even three hundred and twenty-five pounds. He was G.O.'s chief security officer and thought to be in charge of collections.

The BINGO unit knew that it would be difficult, if not impossible, to infiltrate G.O.'s inner circle. Even if it were possible, it would take a considerable amount of time, time the authorities and G.O.'s unwitting victims didn't have. Since time was not in their favor and G.O.'s operations could not be penetrated from the outside, perhaps it could from the inside. The Trojan horse theory. Although the BINGO unit didn't have a Trojan horse, they might be able to cultivate something just as effective.

Barry was shadowed all day and all night for almost a full month. The BINGO unit monitored his every move. They knew his schedule better than even Barry. His habits soon become predictable. It was not long before they determined who his supplier or wholesaler was and on that sultry mid-August evening, Barry was observed and filmed from an unmarked police van making a buy from a mule who they hoped would be more than eager to turn state's evidence in exchange for immunity.

As soon as the money was exchanged for the drugs, the plain clothes detectives descended on Barry and the mule. With guns pointed at Barry, the detectives ordered him face down on the hot pavement and his hands behind his head. When he started to protest, he was told by one of the detectives that he would be shot if he failed to obey their orders.

"Okay! Okay!" was all he said. While one detective held his service weapon trained on Barry's head, the Chameleon handcuffed him. Almost immediately they were joined by other members of the unit.

The CHAMELEON

When Barry was searched it produced all the incriminating evidence the authorities would need to put him away for a decade or two. Not surprisingly, he was more concerned about his step-father's reaction than what the criminal justice system had in store for him. The Chameleon surmised that it would not be long before his withdrawals would leave him craving the crystal meth that fueled his addiction. When 'delirium tremens' (DTs) kicked in, he would worry more about his inevitable involuntary abstinence than even what he could anticipate in the form of retribution from G.O.

And so, the concept of the BINGO unit's version of the Trojan horse was born. It was born out of necessity from the perspectives of both Barry and law enforcement. Although Barry was hostile towards his captors, he had somewhat of an affinity for the Chameleon and even though it wasn't the unit's planned strategy, the Chameleon became the good cop. Seated in one of the interrogation rooms at the CPD, Barry was surrounded by a handful of the most robust in the unit.

Detective Sergeant Wiker Vega read Barry his rights. When Barry said he would only talk to the Chameleon, all were motioned by the Chameleon to leave the room. After the door had been locked behind them, Barry's handcuffs were removed and he requested a cup of coffee. Two cups were brought in, one for Barry, and one for the Chameleon. Sitting on the table was a microphone connected to a digital recorder and to speakers on the wall in the adjacent room where the excluded members of the unit listened and watched through a two-way mirror.

The Chameleon entered the interrogation room and sat down across from Barry. "Barry, when you were first brought into this room you were advised of your constitutional rights. Did you understand those rights?" His voice had a pleasant, friendly tone.

"Yes, this is not the first rodeo and I have been read my Miranda rights."

"You indicated that you would be willing to talk to me. Do you realize that that is something you are not required to do?"

"Of course, but, I have no one else to turn to and…and you remind me of my father who has been deceased now for almost seventeen years." Barry fidgeted in his chair and he studied his thumbs.

"I take it you were close to your father."

"He was my high school civics teacher and our wrestling coach. He made sure I studied and wanted me to be a medical doctor. When he died, I died too. And when my mother married my stepfather, I was led in a different direction and died yet another death."

"Your stepfather is Grundel Ormandi and owner of Barry's Babes & Bar, correct? And I assume the bar was named after you?"

"Correct on both counts. My father left my mother destitute. My mother had gone back to work as a paralegal in a law firm in Los Angeles that specialized in criminal defense work. That's where she met my stepfather, who was a client. She caught his eye and they started dating. He had an automobile dealership there and offered my mother a life style she had never dreamt possible. She was more concerned about raising me than enjoying big houses and fancy cars."

"You strike me as someone with a formal education. Frankly, you're not what I expected."

"I graduated from UCLA with dual majors, philosophy and biology. That was when I planned on being a forensic psychiatrist and before I discovered drugs."

"I take it your introduction to drugs was through your association with your stepfather?"

"In all fairness to Del, as we call him, he tried to keep me away from drugs. It was through working at Triple Bs, however, that I fell in with the wrong crowd. While he and mom went to Europe and I was minding the store while they were gone for two months the summer after college graduation, I got high on alcohol and did my first hit. It was all downhill from there. I've never done anything half-way—as you have already probably gathered," he added miserably.

"I imagine you were a disappointment to your mother."

"Mother was a heavy smoker. She developed lung cancer and passed away shortly after she and Del returned from Europe. Although they didn't actually attribute the lung cancer to her smoking, I'm sure it helped kill her. That was a difficult time for me and for Del, and neither of us has been the same since."

"Does he do drugs?"

"The drugs you saw me purchase tonight were for both of us."

"Because of the amount, I assume you purchased some for resale."

"That was not our regular distributor. But, yes, not all of it was intended for Del and me."

"You seem very cooperative and not at all tentative in talking to me, knowing that all of this is being recorded and could be used against you."

"I guess on some level I was hoping to get busted. I know I've been shadowed and knew I was being shadowed tonight. Things have been happening at Triple Bs that have spiraled out of control—things much more serious than drugs, gambling and prostitution."

"Is that something you want to talk to me about?"

"Ever since Del hired his cousin, Florio Ormandi, I've had little say in the management of Triple Bs and have been relegated to being merely a bouncer. Florio has been doing everything he can to phase me out of the business and even has caused a rift between Del and me, resulting in me having moved out of the family residence. Florio now has my old bedroom."

"What does Del think of that?"

"His health has been declining ever since Florio arrived on the scene, and he seems to be drugged up all the time. I don't think he knows what is going on anymore."

"How long has Florio been running the show?"

"For almost six months now, although he only recently moved his furniture and personal belongings from his home in New Orleans."

"As a law enforcement officer, my main interest is to protect society from the criminal element. Do you understand that?"

"Yes."

"And I can only do that within the bounds of the law."

"Yes, I understand."

"I sense good in you, Barry. I have the feeling that you want to help me do my job. Please tell me I'm not wrong."

"I don't want to end up in a dumpster somewhere being considered a threat and a piece of trash by Florio. One of the strippers at the club has already warned me that I'm on Florio's hit list and that he is in the process of making the funeral arrangements."

"It sounds imminent."

"I know he has had an attorney prepare a will and some powers of attorney for Del to sign. I think I'm safe as long as Del is still alive. When Del is history, I'll be history as well."

"Barry, according to the information we have on you, you've never been convicted of a felony and have never been incarcerated. Although there are some minor offenses on your record, you have an otherwise clean criminal history. Is that accurate?"

"Absolutely, except for my involvement in drugs, and for my involvement at the club, I have been for the most part crime free. However, I am keenly aware that now I will be facing serious felony charges on the possession and possession with intent to distribute illegal drugs."

"Not having been incarcerated, you might not appreciate what it's like to be locked up in a cell not much larger than a clothes closet, with no natural light and surrounded by inmates who would rape you or stab you for an orange."

"Ever since the door was locked behind us, I've been visualizing what it would be like. I remember one time being trapped in a cooler at work when the latch malfunctioned. That was the longest hour of my life. I actually started to cry like a baby, thinking I would not be rescued until morning."

"Barry, I can't promise anything until I talk to the commander. However, I can tell you this. If you can help us put whoever is responsible for the strong-arm tactics being utilized by Triple Bs in collecting on their past due accounts behind bars, we will cut you some slack. Now, in what form that will come I can't say. Depending on your production, it may mean something short of a felony conviction."

"I can help you," Barry said. Burying his head in his hands, he sobbed, "My God, my God!"

It wouldn't be until the next day when Barry's job description would be formulated and a formal agreement entered into between Barry and the CPD and the CCSO. Henceforth, Barry would be referred to by the CPD and the CCSO as the Trojan Horse. Law enforcement now had the inside track.

The CHAMELEON

In the interim, the Chameleon was feeling good about the infiltration into Triple Bs and the conscription of Barry. However, when he finished with Barry and looked at his watch he realized he was already an hour late in picking up Meloni. It was after seven p.m. when he dialed her number. It was unusual for her not to pick up on her cell phone. She'd either not taken it with her to the Kappa Alpha Nu event or had it turned off.

It was with the speed of sound that the Chameleon drove back to the fundraiser. It was already eight-fifteen when he entered the ballroom and dashed on stage to claim the seat in front of the only clean place setting.

Meloni was already at the podium and being handed a plaque with a gavel commemorating her presidency when she spotted the Chameleon. The look of disappointed morphed into delight as she savored the moment. Her dark eyes sparkled as she smiled.

"I've heard it said all my life that all good things come to those who wait. Yet, it is not easy to be patient and sit by idly in eager anticipation for good things to happen. I know that is not and will never be in my nature. However, I've slowly but surely begun to realize that when life appears to be the bleakest, it is usually the prelude to our brightest moments.

"I think there is a flaw in the fable about the lull before the storm. I think it is the other way around. I think more aptly, it is the storm before the serenity, the torrent before the blessings flow. After the darkness there is the light. After the lightning and thunder, there is the rain. After the rain there is the sun. And, at the end of every rainbow there is the treasure to be claimed.

"The Good Book says not to be anxious about anything. But, in everything pray and whatever is true, whatever is noble, whatever is right, whatever is pure, whatever is lovely, and whatever is admirable will transcend all."

The Chameleon knew only too well for whom Meloni's remarks were intended. What intrigued him most, however, were their latent meanings.

CHAPTER EIGHT

Adriana was obviously perplexed and had been crying. Gripping the Chameleon's hands with a sense of some urgency, she led him to the recently reupholstered flowered sofa in the center of her small apartment in Edison Park. There she sat beside him and continued to hold both of his hands tightly in both of hers.

"I just got a call." Her expression was reminiscent of the day of his father's funeral, full of sadness and grief. She bit her lip and blinked away tears.

It hurt him to see her so miserable, since she was ordinarily not one to be overcome by emotion and was strong, especially when confronted by adversity and always in the presence of her sons.

The Chameleon gripped his mother's hand. His heart was racing in fretful expectation.

"Remember me telling you about Lex and Della Stedman?" Adriana asked .

"Of course. They were friends of yours and Dad's when we lived in New York." The Chameleon squinted as if to ask why that mattered.

"The Stedmans were more than just friends," his mother said. "I thought of them as our guardian angels. It was their love, prayers and monthly checks that kept us going all these years. Even though Lex has retired from the FBI and you boys are grown, we are still in touch with one another. Lex and Della still live in the Bronx in the same house near where we used to live. Anyway, Lex has been the FBI's contact with our family since your father's death and is the only one, outside our immediate family, who is aware of our new identity and, of course, our location."

"I remember their Christmas presents when Franc, Tony and I were just kids. We could hardly wait to open their presents, because they were toys and not socks and pajamas."

Now, it was Adriana's turn to squeeze the Chameleon's hand. They laughed and, with the tension somewhat relieved, Adriana continued.

"After Lex and I exchanged pleasantries, I could tell by his voice that it involved your father. He said that he had been contacted by an FBI agent out of the New York Field Office in the Bronx by the name of . . ." Adriana hesitated as she tried to decipher her scribble. Finally, she said, "Trosconi . . . his name is Bruno Trosconi."

Setting the notepad aside, she said, "Trosconi had been hired on at the New York City's main office shortly after your father's death and was assigned the investigation. According to Lex, Trosconi received a telephone call from the doctor of a man who claims to have been responsible for your father's death. Apparently, he had ties with the Mafia at the time and is now on his deathbed at a local hospital and wants to make amends with the authorities, the family of his victim and, of course, his Maker."

"Of course," was all the Chameleon could say, thinking of the killer's motive for making a confession on his deathbed. He had heard little about the circumstances surrounding his father's death and had respected his mother's desire to

106

insulate him and his brothers from those terrible events. He had always wanted to hear what his mother had held secret all those years.

Adriana's face was drawn and her eyes tormented as she began to recount the events that had taken place over forty years before.

"A high-ranking underworld figure by the name of Spizzo "Cobra" Sabineto had been killed in a gang-land slaying in one of the hotels in downtown Manhattan while attending a wedding reception for his niece." His mother repositioned herself on the sofa and looked down at her clasped hands avoiding eye-contact with the Chameleon. "That was in nineteen sixty-five. Your father was thirty-three and had been with the bureau for approximately seven years. He and Lex were assigned to cover the Cobra's funeral at St. Sebastian's Catholic Church in the Bronx. It was their job to report on who came and went and to take photographs of the funeral goers."

Now, lifting her eyes and fixing her gaze directly on her son, she continued. "While taking photographs from a remote location, your father was ambushed and later found slain."

"But . . ." the Chameleon interrupted, "how was he killed? And why?" the Chameleon frowned and shook his head, wondering what had precipitated such an act.

"A knife was found in some shrubs not far from where your father's body was found. The blood on the knife was later established to be his. The 'why' was never determined. However, since his camera and film were nowhere to be found, the speculation at the time was that he had been discovered filming someone not keen with the idea."

"Dad was a rather powerful man," the Chameleon said reflectively. "Whoever did it must have snuck up on him and attacked him from behind. There are not too many that could have overpowered him without some kind of struggle."

"Judging from the condition of your father's clothing, the wounds on his body and the blood and scuff marks on the concrete and surrounding walls, it was evident that your father had been involved in a life-or-death struggle with the assailant." Neither the Chameleon nor his mother could control their emotions any longer and both wept as they envisioned the violent scene and the events that preceded the Chameleon's father's death.

Adriana trembled as the Chameleon held her. "Let's take a break," he said. He led her into the kitchen where he fixed the two of them a cup of hot tea. He continued to hold his mother close as she sipped her tea. It was obvious to the Chameleon that even though his mother must have replayed the gruesome events, as they no doubt unfolded, many times on the screen of her mind, she had not become desensitized and now, subjecting her son to the ordeal, appeared almost too much for her to bear.

The two finished their tea and, before returning to the sitting room, walked out onto the adjoining deck. A breeze ruffled Adriana's hair and sent russet leaves spinning skyward.

"I'm okay now," Adriana said in a subdued voice as she led her son back into the sitting room.

"This can wait," the Chameleon said as he watched his mother amble back to the flowered sofa.

The CHAMELEON

"No," Adriana replied. "The only way you will know about some of these things is if I tell you."

He sat beside her and took her hand again.

"A lot of strange things were discovered following your father's death," Adriana persisted. "Not only had you father's camera and film disappeared but his wallet as well. And, oddly enough, his St. Christopher medal and chain were nowhere to be found. He never took them off, not even when he took a shower. I gave the medal and chain to your father on our wedding day and they are the ones you're now wearing." She then reached over and reverently fingered the medal and chain that hung around the Chameleon's neck.

"Um . . . m . . . m," the Chameleon mumbled and frowned as his mother replaced the medal and chain beneath his shirt collar. "But . . . how?" he asked.

"When you received these from me on the day of your graduation from the police academy, I told you how precious they were and how they should be revered."

"Yes, but how did you get them back?"

"They were given to me personally by the then FBI Director, J. Edgar Hoover. The medal and chain, along with your father's badge and other personal effects, were given to me several months after your father's funeral. I was told that the medal and chain were taken as . . . as a trophy of sorts, much like a scalp, to prove the underworld connection. Apparently, they were mailed to the FBI office in New York City immediately following your father's death."

"It's strange that they weren't kept in evidence in the event of a criminal prosecution."

"Lex informed me that there were no prints or identifying marks on the enclosed items. He said they had been wiped clean. The FBI did keep the packaging, according to Lex, and were checked for prints but with negative results."

"The persons responsible were either very clever or very lucky," the Chamcleon commented. "I don't suppose there were any suspects, let alone arrests."

"No," Adriana replied. "At least not until today when the call came from the hospital."

"Do you want to tell me about Lex Stedman's telephone call?" the Chameleon asked anxiously.

Adriana scanned the notes she had taken at the time of Lex's telephone call. "Lex said that the name of the dying man who claimed to be responsible for your father's death was Gennaro 'Iceman' Orazdenelli. I guess that is how you pronounce his name. Anyway, according to Lex, the man is now in his eighties and claims to have murdered an FBI agent at St. Sebastian's Catholic Church in the Bronx in nineteen sixty-five."

"What does that have to do with us?" the Chameleon asked.

Adriana choked on a sob before replying. "He obviously is talking about the death of your father and wants to talk to a family member no doubt to clear his conscience. Do you want to talk to your father's assassin?"

Full of rage and pent-up hatred, the Chameleon was incensed that the man who showed no mercy all those years ago now wanted mercy. He grimaced as he thought what he would like to do to his father's killer. "Let the demon burn in hell," he said, clenching his teeth and fists. All these years without a father and the unfulfilled longing of his mother and brothers brought a flood of disappointment, frustration, and anguish. It was almost too much for him to handle and would have been impossible if it had not been for his mother who was there to comfort him as she had been all his life.

To find out who killed his father was bittersweet. Now, all he had to do was find out who ordered the hit.

CHAPTER NINE

T he Chameleon had a fitful night and slept little since speaking with Lex Stedman. Now he was ready to board the flight from O'Hare International Airport to La Guardia Airport. La Guardia was closest to the Bronx and Lex would be picking him up at the airport. Lex had said there was some urgency as the Iceman was not long for this world.

Flying over Lake Michigan always intrigued the Chameleon. Its breadth reminded him of the Atlantic Ocean. Its waves were captivating and always hypnotic. He remembered how he and his brothers so loved the beach and their time with their father on the few precious days when their father was not on assignment. He could still picture his father tall, dark and imposing. All the agents were required to be in shape, and his father's physique reminded him of a blown-up version of Rocky Marciano. His father was always measuring his and his brothers' biceps when he came home. The Chameleon wondered what his father would say if he could see him now. The Chameleon was sculpted like his father, and in fact, his mother was always reminding him how much he looked and acted like his father. Nobody kicked sand in the Chameleon's face. Being compared to his father was the ultimate compliment. His father was someone he always sought to emulate.

The Chameleon was not feeling guilty in the least bit about his real intentions in going to the Iceman's bedside. He was not there to give absolution or ratify the heinous acts of a cold-blooded killer who, about to meet his Maker, was seeking forgiveness. Nor was he going out of curiosity to see what his father's executioner looked like. He was there to have the Iceman deliver the crime boss's head on a platter. Once that was determined, he then would "accidently" stand on the Iceman's air hose long enough to hasten his departure into eternal misery without the possibility of parole.

The CHAMELEON

When the Chameleon stepped off of the plane onto the ramp that led to the terminal at La Guardia, he was nervous and eager to shake the hand of the man who was the link to the past, a man who had been a friend and colleague of his father.

Towering over the other passengers as they entered the terminal, the Chameleon spotted a gray-haired man he estimated to be in his mid-seventies and close to the age his father would have been, had he not been killed. The man had a kindly face that bore the signs of a full but stressful existence. In spite of his stooped posture, he seemed proud and alert, squinting as he sized up each arriving passenger. When his eyes met the Chameleon's, he smiled and the Chameleon immediately knew the man was Lex Stedman.

"I'd recognize you anytime, anywhere," Lex said as he peered up at the much taller younger man. "You are the spitting image of your father." Their handshake turned into a tearful embrace.

"You were but a small lad when your father died," Lex said. "The last time I saw you was at your father's funeral."

"That was fifty years ago," the Chameleon said. "I'm guessing you are now in your mid-seventies."

"Actually, I'm seventy-seven. Your father was two years younger than me. God, how I miss him!"

"Me too," the Chameleon said as the two headed for the baggage claim. "That is why I am anxious to talk to the man who claims to have killed him."

As they stood waiting for the carousel to rotate, the Chameleon asked, "Do you know anything about this man you referred to as the Iceman or his background?"

"If you're asking me if it is possible the Iceman was the one who killed your father, then I would have to say yes." Folding his arms and hesitating for a moment, Lex finally added, "Although reputedly he was just a small-time hood, the FBI had their sights on him long before your father's death. He was suspected in several unsolved gangland executions. NCIC doesn't show any felony convictions."

"Does the Iceman know I am coming?" the Chameleon asked.

"Both his doctor and the bureau have been told only that a relative of your father would be arriving. Not even Bruno Trosconi, at this point, knows your true identity. As far as he and everyone else knows, you are Chris Carcelli, a detective with the Chicago Police Department and somehow related."

"When we spoke by telephone last night, you mentioned that the FBI was still involved in the investigation into the unsolved death of my father."

"The slaying of an FBI agent is not something that is ever placed on the backburner. Even though your father was killed in nineteen sixty-five, it's still an open case—one that I continue to be involved in despite my retirement."

"For that, we are grateful," the Chameleon said as he squeezed Lex's forearm.

Lex's eyes moistened and his lips quivered. "Your father was not just my partner and my friend, but he was like a brother to me. I

think of him every day and pray for him and your
family every night when I say the rosary."

Lex drove like a man possessed, even
though traffic from La Guardia was heavy. The
Chameleon held on as the car swayed and swerved
toward St. Bartholomew's Hospital where the
Iceman lay dying. *Would they be there in time?*

Walking into the Iceman's hospital room
was almost surreal. So much had happened so
quickly that the Chameleon wondered if it wasn't
still part of the nightmare he had awakened from
the night before. He always had a picture of a man
in his mind, though fuzzy, of his father's killer.
The pathetic, frail figure lying on the semi-
elevated hospital bed in front of him somehow
did not fit the preconceived mold.

The CHAMELEON

A skull with dark, stretched skin revealing furrows of a hard life and challenging last days was dominated by hollow, expressionless eyes. His nose was distorted as if it had been broken many times. The old man's mouth bore the archaic remnants of teeth that had never met a dentist or been introduced to a toothbrush. The Chameleon thought, *God, he looks like a mummy!*

Upon seeing the Chameleon, the Iceman looked as if he had seen a ghost. His eyes widened. His jaw dropped. He just stared at the Chameleon through milky, rheumy eyes. Then, with a weak gesture, he lifted a frail, trembling hand laced with purple veins and paper thin flesh, and motioned the Chameleon to his side. Obliging, the Chameleon drew near. The Iceman then reached towards the top of the Chameleon's open sport shirt and slowly retrieved the St. Christopher medal. His mouth formed the words, "My God," and he whispered something in Italian. His mouth quivered and his eyes pleaded with the Chameleon as he murmured, "Forgive me."

Expressionless, the Chameleon looked into the eyes of the Iceman and asked, "Who killed my father?"

Gasping for air, the Iceman said "M-me."

"No, I want to know *who* ordered it?" the Chameleon demanded in a hushed but desperate tone.

The Iceman's eyes rolled back. With his dying breath, he whispered "D . . . O . . . J." In one word and an acronym, he had solved the mystery surrounding the execution of the FBI agent at St. Sebastian's Catholic Church in the Bronx some fifty years before.

The monitor began to squeal as the patient flat-lined and alarms sounded. A doctor rushed in followed by a cadre of nurses and attendants who began checking for vitals.

"I'm sorry. He's gone," the doctor announced, noting the time of death.

A nurse pulled the sheet up over the dead man's head as Lex and the Chameleon left the room.

Commandeering a vacant conference room adjacent to the hospital chapel, Lex and the Chameleon sat opposite each other at the large oak table equipped to seat twenty. Stunned and incredulous, the Chameleon, still shaking said, "I can't believe the Department of Justice would have an FBI agent assassinated, let alone hire the Mafia to do it."

Looking around as if to make sure the doors where closed and that the walls didn't have ears, Lex said, "I don't care if I get in trouble for breaking my oath of confidentiality. Besides, there isn't a lot the bureau can do to me except terminate my retirement and cancel my insurance.

"To begin with, DOJ does not stand for Department of Justice, at least not in the context in which the Iceman used it. DOJ has had a much different reference, or at least in the past, among the underworld. DOJ has reference to what has been referred to as a tribunal that was established in the 1960s to handle disputes between crime families and mobsters. DOJ stands for Dispenser of Justice.

"In the pre-nineteen-sixties, Lex continued, "the feuds among crime organizations and among members within the various organizations resulted in a high casualty count. The mindset then was to administer justice, or at least perceived justice, and then ask questions later. A misunderstanding could erupt into a full-blown war in a matter of days. To dissipate rather than escalate became the desired method of avoiding extinction.

"Anyway, the tribunal approach was reputedly the brainchild of a law school dropout who later became what one might call the chief arbitrator or mediator. Actually, the Dispenser of Justice was the title given to this mastermind when, in reality, the tribunal was composed of three individuals who were selected from among the crime families who had formed this Mafia cartel.

"The tribunal was run much like the courts," Lex continued, "and the disputes were resolved in much the same fashion. The tribunal had the power to administer punishment like our criminal courts, except that it was not long before the tribunal was consumed with its own power and became a kangaroo court of sorts and embarked on some witch hunts that hit close to home. Those mob bosses and their mob families who were not members of the cartel received some very unfavorable treatment, and it was not long before anonymous whistleblowers were emerging from all corners of the state. The tribunal and their methods were compromising the mob creed and the iron-clad code of allegiance and silence.

"To this day, little is known about this highly secret tribunal. The name of the mastermind still remains a mystery. Retribution for disclosure was always the main impediment against detection. Most, if not all individuals, close to the mobs would deny it ever existed. In its heyday, it is thought to have ordered the execution of some very high-ranking government officials, key law enforcement personnel, and anyone and everyone perceived to be an enemy of the Mafia. Today is the first I've learned of its supposed connection to your father's death."

"Are any of the members of the tribunal known to the FBI?" the Chameleon asked.

"As I said, the tribunal has, to our knowledge, been a relic of the past for over twenty-five years. Personally, I doubt the bureau was ever privy to the identities of the members of the tribunal. However, I'll do some nosing around and see what I can turn up. It's too bad we didn't have access to the Iceman before. What he told us obviously has been a carefully guarded secret."

"How can we be sure what the Iceman told us is factual?"

Lex scowled. "We can't. The Iceman worked under a number of bosses during his career in crime and even though he was subpoenaed before various federal grand juries, he never fingered anyone. That may be the reason he lived so long. His convictions were petty and he pretty much stayed one step ahead of the law. Although his signature was thought to appear on various gang-land slayings from time to time, there was never any real proof and, as the saying goes, dead men don't talk. For a hit man to be known as deadly, silent, indiscriminate, innocuous and undetectable was job security and the Iceman, to my knowledge, never filed nor needed to file for unemployment compensation. To specifically answer your question, I would say he was telling the truth."

"We would certainly hope that a man who was seconds away from judgment would tell the truth. He wouldn't have implicated himself and then lied about from whom he received his orders. It's too bad for him and for us that his time expired before he could tell all."

"As I said earlier, dead men don't talk. Not even a federal grand jury could get him to say more. We're fortunate he told us as much as he did."

"It's too bad," the Chameleon said, "because I only had one more question to ask and he only had one more answer we needed. Who specifically gave the order?"

"Hopefully, he will speak to us from the grave," Lex said, suspecting the Iceman's secret had been buried with him forever.

CHAPTER TEN

Lex was unable to put names and faces to the Mafia tribunal. Being nameless and faceless, the members of the tribunal were isolated against detection and prosecution. Even if they were identifiable, the information provided by the Iceman would be considered inadmissible, incompetent and insufficient in a court of law. But, since this was not a court of law, even a hint would be more than what they had.

Coming into the Lake Tahoe Basin for the first time is breath-taking. It is bordered by the lush Sierra Mountains on the west, and the Carson

Range on the east. Tahoe is the second deepest lake in the United States, and was once one of the purest lakes in the country. The white sand beaches and crystal blue water make people believe they have just arrived at the shores of the Mediterranean. It is the home and playground of the rich and poor alike. About a third of the lake lies in Nevada, and the rest in California. The Nevada side of the lake boasts Incline Village and Heavenly ski resorts, as well as the clubs and casinos at North Shore and South Shore.

Along the west shore are numerous hamlets, Emerald Bay, beaches, campgrounds, Vikingsholm and it is only a short distance to Northstar and Squaw Valley ski resorts. It is a unique and uniquely beautiful place.

As the CHC&R's private Airstream jet, dropped into the basin and landed in the narrow airport at South Tahoe, Adriana pressed her nose against the porthole trying to drink it all in. September at Lake Tahoe is thought by some to be the most remarkable time of the year. It is a place that truly exemplifies the discernible changes in the passing of the seasons. The cool crispness of autumn marks the end of summer and the anticipated influx of skiers a couple months away.

Carleono Baranetti's sprawling estate and luxury Holiday Casino & Resort sat less than five miles apart at South Shore Lake on the Nevada side of the lake. Other than the Nevada Gaming Control Board and Magdalena, his wife of almost forty-four years, Carleono was answerable to no one.

As they deplaned, Meloni, the Chameleon and Adriana were met at the airport by a limousine and greeted by both Carleono and Magdalena. The Chameleon observed the interaction between Meloni and her parents. It was obvious Meloni was the love of their lives. Even though it had not been that long since they had last seen each other, they cried and hugged as though it had been a lifetime.

It was not long before Carleono's and Magdalena's attention was focused on the Chameleon and his mother. Meloni started the introductions first with Adriana.

"This is Chris' mother, Adriana," she said as she put her arm around Adriana's shoulder.

"Did you say mother or sister?" Carleono asked as he held Adriana's outstretched hand in both of his. Adriana beamed and then responded to Magdalena's warm embrace.

"This is my friend Chris," Meloni said as she placed her arm around the Chameleon's waist. The two men shook hands and so did the Chameleon and Meloni's mother.

"Go on and hug him, Mother," Meloni coaxed. "He won't bite!" The two then gave each other a hug.

"I can see where Meloni gets her looks," the Chameleon commented nodding in Magdalena's direction.

"From both sides of the family, it appears," Adriana added as Carleono smiled approvingly.

While Carleono's driver, aided by the Sky Cap, stowed the baggage in the back of the limo, Carleono and the Chameleon assisted the ladies into the large, comfortable passenger compartment. They all settled inside and Carleono began pouring drinks.

"I see everyone has found the ice cubes and beverages," the limo driver observed as he began closing the limo's doors. Hesitating momentarily, he added, "The compartment next to the fridge contains some delectables the

Baranetti's chef insisted be included. Enjoy! Be sure to buckle up." He then closed the doors and climbed into the driver's seat.

Adriana looked at the Chameleon and raised her eyebrows. "Quite the life," she whispered to the Chameleon as everyone adjusted their seatbelts.

As they exited the airport, Carleono lifted his glass. "Meloni tells me you're a detective with the Chicago Police Department."

The Chameleon nodded.

"I've always been interested in law enforcement. In fact, I wanted to be a federal prosecutor when I was very young. If it hadn't been for my fraternity brothers and all the distractions, I would have finished law school." He drank deeply from his glass and smacked his lips. "I was a big disappointment to my father who came to this country from Italy as a teenager. He wanted me to be either a priest or a lawyer."

The Chameleon laughed. "From what I have been told, you went into something a lot more respectable and lucrative. In recent years, lawyers and priests have had a lot of explaining to do. Their reputations, it appears, have been irreparably tarnished."

"If you had become a priest," Magdalena reminded, "we wouldn't be sitting here today with our precious daughter and her wonderful friends."

"That's probably true in theory," Carleono replied sarcastically, studying the ice in his glass. "But I'm disappointed in all the people in whom we place all our trust, including our clergy, politicians and governmental officials, who are as bad as or worse than those they badger."

"I'm with you there," Adriana said.

Meloni just snuggled next to the Chameleon. "Hope you enjoy your stay at my parents' little cottage," she whispered into the Chameleon's ear.

The chauffeur drove through the slow moving traffic that was the norm for nearly anywhere along the lake these days. They passed Carleono's Holiday Casino & Resort standing brilliant white like the sand on the shore. The casino was done in Roman architecture with statues perched along the edge of a huge reflecting pool and water feature. At the end of the reflecting pool was a larger than life-sized sculpture of a Roman soldier in a chariot behind a team of galloping horses. The statue was brilliant gold that gleamed in the bright sunlight. Huge electronic signs announced that Celine Dion was the current attraction appearing on stage. Adriana gawked as the limo proceeded through South Shore, finally turning into a manicured drive and through a massive set of gates leading into the Carleono estate.

The beautiful, sprawling home rose up before them with the brilliant blue of the lake behind it. The estate was colossal by anyone's standards and every bit as impressive as its Roman counterparts from which the CHC&R had been inspired. It reminded the Chameleon very much of Caesar's Palace in Las Vegas. Taking advantage of the vast expanse of the body of water to the west, it was as if the CHC&R was located near the Tyrrhenian Sea. It certainly had an authentic Roman flavor with the sweeping arches, long verandas flanked by fluted balustrades, pillars, fountains and sculpted grounds. It was not a paradise lost but a paradise discovered and cultivated.

The Baranetti "cottage," with its sleek yacht moored in the slip at the end of a long dock adjacent to the "backyard," was not quite as large as the Palazzo di Montecitorio in Rome, but almost. If he had not already passed Carleono's Casino, the Chameleon would have thought that this *was* the casino. He was glad he was not the one paying the withholding tax on the fulltime staff that they met upon their arrival, nor the utility bills. Meloni had not prepared him for this. In some ways, he felt intimidated.

The guest quarters were larger than the penthouse suites at luxury hotels. He guessed he could slum it in such a cottage. Instead of her usual private quarters, Meloni insisted that she be placed in the same wing as the Chameleon and his mother. *Quite a change from our apartments back home*, the Chameleon thought.

The Chameleon was quickly introduced to a lifestyle reserved only for the very rich and privileged. After they got settled, he and his mother were treated like royalty. They were outfitted with items from the boutiques and shops that adorned the main halls of CHC&R. With

Meloni's taste and discernment, the Chameleon could now easily be mistaken for a movie star or professional athlete—except on the private golf course and tennis court, where his deception in short order would be exposed.

As an undercover officer, he played a lot of roles and bit parts. In the past, he could pretend to be someone he wasn't. However, here with all the pomp and pageantry fit for a king, he felt uncomfortable. He had not grown up in opulence. It was foreign to him. Upon meeting Meloni, he had been himself, promising that as between the two, there would be no pretense or game playing. Their relationship was too valuable to be otherwise. Now, he found himself in a compromising situation. To some it would appear to be a dream come true, but to him, it was a nightmare.

Growing up with two brothers was a time fraught with daydreaming and fantasies. He dreamt of being a famous astronaut, especially after visiting NASA while on a family trip to Houston. His brother Franc was going to be a movie star in the mold of John Wayne, and later, Troy Donahue, a 1960's heart-throb. In fact,

Franc had done some stunt riding for Warner Brothers Studio the summer after his sophomore year in college. He still owned a stable of Arabians, which he liked to train and ride. Tony, on the other hand, was going to be a famous rock star and thought he had died and gone to heaven when their mother allowed him to switch from piano to guitar. Though a gifted composer, he had long since abandoned his aspiration.

Being the oldest son and becoming fatherless at the age of seven, the Chameleon had become the father figure. That was something that was not conferred but assumed. He relished being the man of the house and making life easier for his mother and brothers. Realizing now how Meloni was raised, he now felt emasculated. He could never offer her this life and he began to doubt himself. *To lose one's own self-respect is to lose everything.* He was determined not to let that happen.

Despite the effort to make him feel welcome, the Chameleon had a miserable time at Lake Tahoe and was only too eager to return to familiar turf and his accustomed life style. He felt he had masked his consternation rather well, but that his paranoia, no doubt, had distorted his thinking. At no time was he ever made to feel that Meloni was selecting her own father over him. In fact, it was just the opposite. She seemed to ignore everyone and everything and concentrated her full attention on him. His possessiveness and insecurity he hoped would not be his undoing. He had found someone who loved him as much as he loved her and he was not anxious to throw it all away. Not this time.

CHAPTER ELEVEN

It was not difficult for the Chameleon to understand the concept behind the tribunal. He remembered a discussion at the police academy about organized crime that the Mafia was actually organized in the seventeenth century to fight the war against tyranny and corruption. It had been a noble cause by a noble organization. However, its focus changed in short order, much like the noble quest of the tribunal changed from solving problems to creating problems. Its intended purpose was unification; instead it became divisive and oppressive. The Chameleon thought this somewhat ironic, since the word *mafia* was derived from an Arabic word meaning *union*.

The Chameleon would have to admit, if he were to bare his soul, that he was both impressed with and intimidated by Carleono. Carleono was dignified and self-assured but not arrogant or conceited, knowledgeable and wise but not dogmatic or authoritative, thoughtful and discerning but not stubborn or bigoted, and sensible and reflective but not unreasonable and trifling.

It was not difficult to admire self-made men, especially those who rose from obscurity to prominence by beating the odds. Survival of the fittest was one thing but to become the best of the best was something else. For someone like Bill Gates to become the wealthiest man in the universe, hop-scotching the wealthiest of the wealthy, especially in a relatively short period of time, was still an enigma to the Chameleon that defied all logic. After being exposed to Carleono's vast empire, the Chameleon was now experiencing a similar awe for Carleono.

Over the years, the Chameleon had heard something that now kept echoing in his mind: *Behind every great fortune is a great crime.* Even though he had been in law enforcement for almost thirty years and been involved in the investigation of blue-collar and white-collar crimes, he did not believe that to be altogether true. And, it was obviously not true in Bill Gates' case. However, with the passing of each day and the corporate scandals that were coming to light, he was admittedly becoming somewhat of a cynic.

When they had settled in for drinks before dinner, Adriane dusted off her interviewing skills. Both she and the Chameleon were skeptical as to how Carleono had amassed his fortune and now was as good a time as any to probe. "So, tell me, Mr. Baranetti, how did you get your start?"

"When you address me as Mr. Baranetti, I think you are referring to my father. We should be on a first name basis by this time. Just call me Carleono or, as Mags does, Carley. And, I hope you don't mind if we call you Adriana?"

"No, not at all," Adriana said blushing.

"Where would you like for me to start?"

"On the drive from the airport, I heard you mention to Chris that your parents were from Italy. My grandparents also emigrated from Italy."

"Oh, what part?" Carleono asked.

"Both sets were from Northern Italy and spent their married life in Florence. How about your parents?"

"They came from opposite ends of Italy. My father was born and raised in Turin. My mother was born near the island of Capri close to the entrance to the Bay of Naples. Are you familiar with the Isle of Capri?"

"Am I *familiar* with the Isle of Capri?" Carleono asked gesturing with his open hands. "Hell, we own a hotel there and go back and forth at least once a year. How about you? Have you been to Capri?"

"The summer before Chris' father died, the five of us spent two weeks in Italy and stayed several nights on Provinciale Marina Grande."

"Provinciale Marina Grande? The hotel I inherited from my uncle is located on Provinciale Marina Grande. It wasn't the Hotel Villa Baranetti where you stayed, was it?"

"I don't think so, although your last name did sound familiar when I was introduced to Meloni and she mentioned her maiden name."

"The HVB is as old as the island itself. It's been remodeled a number of times over the years. It is very possible that you stayed there."

"Here, let me have Riccardi freshen our drinks," the Chameleon said as he collected the glasses. He hurried as he was interested in the conversation between Carleono and his mother and didn't want to miss anything. Meloni assisted.

"Were you also born in Italy?" Adriana asked.

"I was born in Capri in July of nineteen hundred and twenty-four, two years after my parents married. I would have been barely a year old when my parents came to America."

"Did your family have relatives already living in this country?"

"My Uncle Nick, my father's older brother, had settled in the New York area sometime in nineteen-o-five, having emigrated from Italy at the age of nineteen. My father worked for Uncle Nick upon his arrival and ultimately went in business with him."

"It must have been difficult for the Baranetti's to get established in a new country with few contacts and having to learn English."

"Uncle Nick had already been in America some twenty years before we arrived. Back then, it was certainly a land of opportunity. Uncle Nick took advantage of every opportunity. He had the Midas touch."

"Thank you, Chris," Carleono said as the Chameleon handed him a fresh drink. He then took a sip and said, "Where was I?"

"You were talking about your Uncle Nick," Adriana replied.

"Oh yes," Carleono said as he set down his drink.

"Uncle Nick was very enterprising. Shortly after his arrival in New York, he was befriended by an old established family and was able to borrow what in those days was considered large sums of money. In nineteen hundred and thirty-eight, when Uncle Nick was forty-nine, he purchased a dilapidated building in the vicinity of Yankee Stadium and turned it into what would become known as the Baranetti Saloon and much later Baranetti's Sport Bar & Grill, a notorious watering hole for Yankee players and fans. That was in nineteen thirty-eight and Uncle Nick was forty-nine at the time.

"Two years later, Uncle Nick purchased a fledgling clothing store, which became the forerunner of Baranetti Mercantile Company. There, my father learned the trade and later managed and ultimately owned Baranetti Mercantile Company. It became a very successful enterprise and my father eventually added two more branches in the city."

"Meloni had mentioned you had a younger brother who lives in Cleveland. Is he your only sibling?"

"I had two brothers. I say *had* because my brother, Stefano, who was two years younger than me was killed in the line of duty during World War II. The brother who lives in Cleveland is five years younger than me. His name is Gilberto and he recently turned the operation of his five automobile dealerships in Ohio over to his two sons."

"It doesn't sound like you're ready to retire."

"I still have much to do before I call it quits. If I'd become a lawyer, as my family wanted, I would have been able to hang it up a long time ago."

"Speaking of being a lawyer, what happened to cause you to drop out of law school?"

Carleono fidgeted with the stem of his martini glass. "The truth is that I flunked out, plain and simple. I was too busy with other things and didn't concentrate on my studies. It's something I regret. My parents were not too pleased. They wondered how their son, having graduated with honors from Fordham University with a business degree, couldn't get Cs in law school."

"What year did you graduate from Fordham?"

"That was in nineteen-forty-six. I was twenty-two at the time."

"A degree in business apparently has held you in good stead all these years."

"Actually, it was the skills I learned from my father and Uncle Nick, by working for and with them in their various businesses that gave me the edge. Being exposed at an early age to the tavern business and its side operations are what allowed me to turn Baranetti's Sport Bar & Grill into a money-making machine. I got my break when Uncle Nick's emphysema caused him to turn the business over to me."

"You ended up owning Baranetti's Sport Bar & Grill?"

"When Uncle Nick passed away in nineteen-fifty at the age of sixty-one, I inherited his entire estate which was sizable at the time. Uncle Nick had never married and I was, in essence, his adopted son. So, at age twenty-six, I was a millionaire with everything that went with it."

"I'll bet Baranetti's Sport Bar & Grill was a goldmine being located where it was?"

"As I said, it was a money-making machine and is to this day. With what it generated and what I inherited from Uncle Nick, Baranetti Enterprises, Inc. was formed and within less than twenty years controlled businesses in all of the boroughs of New York City–Manhattan, Queens, Brooklyn, Staten Island and, of course, the Bronx."

"Was everything centered in New York City?"

"No, BEI had satellites in upstate New York: Buffalo, Rochester, Syracuse and Albany. Years later, we expanded into several of the adjoining states."

"How did you and Magdalena meet?"

Carleono beamed at Magdalena. "I was watching the Miss America pageant on television in nineteen-sixty-three with my brother, Gilberto, when I fell in love with the contestant from New York. I made the vow then-and-there that someday Magdalena Bellerosa would be the next

Mrs. Carleono Baranetti. You can guess the rest of the story."

Adriana was troubled with the reference to the next Mrs. Carleono Baranetti. "If my math is correct, you were in your forties when you married Magdalena."

"Thirty-nine to be exact. In my early thirties, for a brief period of time, I had been married, or so I thought, to a dancer in one of my clubs. The marriage, however, was annulled when I discovered that she had not been officially divorced from her previous spouse, a broker on Wall Street."

When it was announced that dinner was being served, Carleono sighed and looked at Adriana. "Saved by the bell!"

As they walked towards the dining room, Magdalena pulled Adriana aside and said quietly, "Carley really opened up to you. He told you in one hour more than he has told me in a half-century." Adriana smiled and shrugged.

At dinner, the Chameleon was seated between Meloni and Magdalena. It was there that Magdalena captured the Chameleon's admiration and affection.

CHAPTER TWELVE

On a wintery day in December, three months after his trip to Lake Tahoe, with the wind carrying the chill from Lake Michigan in his direction, the Chameleon fielded a long-distance telephone call from the FBI field office in the Bronx. "Chris," Lex said, "I am here with Bruno Trosconi, the agent who contacted me when the Iceman wanted to make his deathbed confession. We have you on a speakerphone."

"Hi, Chris," the other voice said. "I am Bruno Trosconi. We have never met, but I worked with Lex and your father and am still the lead investigator in attempting to identify and bring to justice those responsible for your father's death."

"I appreciate that very much, Mr. Trosconi," the Chameleon said. "It is good to

148

speak with you. Lex said you could be trusted with my true identity."

"Absolutely," Bruno replied, "but please, call me Bruno."

"Bruno has done some extensive investigation on the Iceman," Lex interjected. "He has been able to piece together the Iceman's work-history and by whom the Iceman was employed, at least around the time your father was killed. Here, let me have Bruno tell you."

"We have collected governmental records from various agencies located in the State of New York during the year of your father's death," Bruno began. "We have come up with some very telling information. In nineteen sixty-five, a Gennaro Orazdenelli also known as the Iceman, age thirty-six, had been employed by Baranetti's Sport Bar & Grill in the Bronx. The owner on the liquor licenses found in the archives was listed as Carleono Baranetti."

The Chameleon could scarcely believe his ears. "Carleono—Carleono Baranetti?" he managed to murmur. That was not a name that was easily mistakable.

"Yes, Carleono Baranetti," Bruno repeated. "Do you recognize the name?"

"You might say I do," the Chameleon said, trying to regain composure. "Does he have a rap sheet?"

Bruno responded, "The only Baranetti with a rap sheet is a Nicoletti Baranetti who was born February 8, 1889. Nicoletti's arrests and convictions were for petty gambling violations. No felonies."

"There were a number of well-known underworld figures who hung around and were connected to Baranetti's Sport Bar & Grill in the 1950s and 1960s," Lex interrupted. "With its proximity to Yankee Stadium, its suspected gaming operation and glamorous women performers, it was *the* hot spot. Even proprietors of its competitors hung out there. It was the place to be and the place to be seen."

"How might that be relevant?" the Chameleon asked Lex.

"The year that your father was killed, our bureau chief sent your father and me to a highly sensitive meeting attended by the NYPD Chief of Police, a well-respected man by the name of Medwell Dyer. The chief had received a report that three of the members of the detective squad were on the take and on the payroll of Carleono Baranetti. He didn't want to handle it internally, for obvious reasons, and was requesting assistance from the FBI. At first we thought it to be outside our jurisdiction, but later determined that the payoffs came from a bank in the state of Illinois. Because of the interstate nature, it was thought to be in our bailiwick.

"Anyway, your father and I were assigned to the case and with some ridiculous disguises, began frequenting Baranetti's Sport Bar & Grill and managed to gamble away several thousand dollars of the government's precious 'buy money.' On several occasions, we were asked to join Carleono Baranetti for drinks and were guests for dinner on one occasion in his private dining hall. As far as he knew, we were legitimate employees of a brokerage firm on Wall Street. He was always very cordial and eager to relieve us of our money.

"In no time, we would observe one or two and even sometimes all three of the suspected members of the NYPD. Our disguises must not have been very effective, at least not your father's, as on the weekend of our second week undercover, your father was recognized by one of the detectives. That was a risk we took when investigating fellow law enforcement officers. It's impossible to work together and attend law enforcement conferences and seminars together without becoming familiar with each other.

"I still remember the name of that detective, even after all of these years. His name was Vittorio Ancona. He was killed while making a drug bust some years later. The circumstances were very suspicious and no suspects were ever found. It's strange I would still remember his name. Maybe his face is etched in my mind because of the encounter that night at Baranetti's Sport Bar & Grill when he recognized us, or at least your father. It scared the hell out of both your father and me.

"Early the following Monday, we were called into the bureau chief's office and met by the commander of the three suspected detectives. The commander was livid about us having tailed his fine and upstanding men and thus impugning the integrity of his department. In essence, he told us to buzz off. We were barking up the wrong tree, and, they were working undercover. Our chief then rescinded our assignment and reassigned us to other duty."

The Chameleon was trying to absorb everything, especially Carleono's possible connection to his father's death. He was still in shock and said little. He wasn't sure where all of this was leading but could see the writing starting to appear on the wall.

Lex seemed eager to talk. "Your father was stubborn and he continued investigating despite the chief's orders, my pleading and his better judgment. None of us, especially your father, liked bad cops. He was determined to pin the goods on the three he was convinced were on the take.

"I was the only one at the bureau who knew what your father was doing. He, of course, would confide in me and keep me posted. He had developed a source who apparently had been married to Carleono's first wife. The source was a stock broker on Wall Street. Being unhappy with Carleono, the stock broker was more than willing to spill his guts. His wife had worked for Carleono before marrying him and Carleono apparently kept few secrets. He supposedly became privy to many of Carleono's deep dark secrets.

"Your father apparently was making some very important people nervous. It was not long before he was beginning to receive death threats. However, he was not dissuaded in the least. On the morning of his death, he had called and said it was urgent that we talk. We had arranged to meet after the funeral of Spizzo Sabineto and discuss a dilemma he was facing with regard to the errant detectives. He apparently was seeking my advice. He never made it past St. Sebastian's Catholic Church. What he knew obviously died with him.

"He had given me the name and contact information for his stock broker informant. I never was able to utilize the information because the stock broker was found floating face down in the East River the day after your father was killed."

"Do you think there was a connection?" the Chameleon asked.

"You mean between the death of your father and his informant, or between the death of your father and Carleono Baranetti?" Lex asked.

Hesitating for a moment and biting his bottom lip, the Chameleon reflectively said, "both."

"Carleono is a very powerful man and certainly was in 1965. His tentacles, and thus his sphere of influence, reached some lofty places far beyond the three detectives. It is certainly more than a coincidence that the detectives' commander interceded for his men and caused the investigation to come to a standstill. Your father's persistence obviously was perceived as a threat and he was no doubt tailed, resulting in the discovery of the stock broker connection. It was an inescapable conclusion, therefore, that your father and his informant be eliminated to protect the integrity and safety of the Baranetti organization. For them it was an easy tradeoff. Everyone but them was indispensable."

"It is obvious dead men don't talk. Carleono must have had some pretty effective ears in high places especially the NYPD. And he probably paid a pretty penny for the info."

"Absolutely right," Lex responded. "It is obvious that the reason the police raids never produced anything of an incriminatory nature at any of Carleono's establishments was because Carleono was always tipped off."

"Either that or he was clairvoyant," the Chameleon chided.

"Or, maybe both," Bruno chuckled.

"And that he went all those years with not so much as a traffic infraction, boggles the mind," the Chameleon said. "Carleono must have either been a saint, a miracle worker or a magician."

"In addition to being a clairvoyant," Lex added.

After hanging up the telephone, the Chameleon ruminated over the revelation. He concluded that his father had stumbled upon some very sensitive, and no doubt incriminating, evidence that was perceived as a vital threat to the Baranetti organization. Somehow the discovery was leaked to Carleono, either directly or indirectly. Knowing that Donato Leonardo Mira, the Chameleon's father, could not be bought off, he resorted to the most serious and permanent alternative. And, there was only one effective way to permanently silence the stock broker. The Iceman was no doubt commissioned to perform both tasks. The Chameleon knew first hand that that was the case, at least in regard to his father.

The Chameleon was bothered by the fact that the Iceman had fingered the Dispenser of Justice, not Carleono Baranetti personally. Could they be one and the same? Lex had said the tribunal sought to eradicate those perceived to be a threat to the Mafia, including law enforcement personnel, which included the FBI and thus his father. To protect the Mafia and his own fiefdom, Carleono no doubt had ordered the hit. The Chameleon knew that to think that that was the case was one thing, but to prove it was something entirely different. And if it was proven, then what? That was as big a quandary, maybe even bigger than the conundrum they now faced.

CHAPTER THIRTEEN

I t was another blustery day in Chicago, and the Chameleon wondered if that December Tuesday might not have set a record for the coldest day for that date. He guessed it was the coldest spot in the nation and at least ten degrees colder than even Frasier or Gunnison, Colorado. The Chameleon was thinking that his brother Franc's invitation to spend Christmas with him and his family in Coral Gables, Florida, might not be such a bad offer after all.

The maxim that a leopard doesn't change its spots certainly applied to the Chameleon again this year. Despite his good intentions, he had waited until the last minute to do his Christmas shopping. It was already the eleventh and he had not purchased gift one. Deciding what to buy for his mother was always problematic, but his dilemma was compounded this year by what to purchase for Meloni. He couldn't compete at the level of her parents and if he could he would be buying her a new Mercedes to match each color in the rainbow.

In less than forty-five minutes, he would be meeting Meloni at her shop. She would help him make the family selections and then they would be having lunch at Diego's Mexican Restaurant. Although they had talked on the telephone, this would be the first time they would be in each other's company since the distressing telephone call of Lex Stedman and Bruno Trosconi from the FBI office in New York City.

The Chameleon was feeling guilty about prejudging Meloni's father. He knew everyone was clothed with the presumption of innocence and before determining guilt the accuser should be convinced of the guilt of the accused beyond a reasonable doubt. In the Chameleon's eyes, however, it was evident that the road of guilt led to Carleono. Carleono had the means, motive and the opportunity, and the confessed killer had been his employee.

There was another critical piece of evidence that connected Carleono to his father's death of which not even Lex was aware, something that the Chameleon deliberately withheld. Lex had said the Mafia tribunal was the brainchild of a law school dropout whose name was unknown. By Carleono's own admission, he had dropped out of law school before the end of his first year. He was in New York in 1965 and could easily have been the one the Iceman referred to as the Dispenser of Justice.

The Chameleon could not overcome that tugging feeling of guilt that he somehow was being disloyal to Meloni. It mattered not what her father had done, even as grievous as it was, as far as his feelings for Meloni was concerned. Meloni was not, nor should she be, responsible for the sins of her father. She had some of his DNA but that did not mean she had inherited his conscience or lack thereof. In fact, she was the epitome of all that was good, wholesome and pure. By condemning Carleono, he was in no way condemning Meloni.

Having lunch at Diego's was becoming an almost weekly occurrence. Diego's had an authentic Mexican menu, and an atmosphere and chefs that made it a five-star restaurant. By now, the waiters and waitresses knew Meloni and the Chameleon by their Mexican names, Melanita and Cristobal, and made every effort to seat them at their favorite table.

Toasting a margarita *con limon verde* and celebrating the Chameleon's triumph in the purchase of the consummate Christmas gifts for his mother and daughters–thanks to Meloni's discerning taste and wise selections–the two were eager to make up for lost time.

"You seem preoccupied, Superman," Meloni said. "What's wrong?"

I think your father had my father killed, he wanted to say. If there was ever a time to be totally candid with Meloni, pour out his heart and seek her sage advice, it was now. Discretion was the better part of valor, however. To rush to rashness and make bold assertions and accusations

161

that for the most part were unsubstantiated would most certainly result in the ruination of their relationship. That was something he did not want to risk nor did he want to inflict on her the accompanying anguish that would inevitably flow from it.

"I'm trying to solve the riddle of a particularly sensitive and perplexing matter that I wish I could share with you," the Chameleon said reflectively.

"Is it something I can help you with?" Meloni asked softly.

"Not right now, but maybe someday," he replied.

With tears forming and torment reflecting from his deep, soulful eyes, he reached for Meloni's hands. Clasping his, Meloni conveyed with expression and touch that she was inextricably intertwined in his spirit and wherever he was mentally, spiritually and physically, there she would be with him also.

"I love you," she whispered into his ear.

"I love you, too," he whispered back as her warm moist lips met his. It was at that moment, the Chameleon determined irrevocably the Christmas gift he would be purchasing for the melody of his heart.

It was not something he particularly wanted to discuss with his mother, but he felt compelled to do so. As dispassionately as he could, he would describe the telephone conversation he had had with Lex Stedman and Bruno Trosconi. Now that he had collected and connected the dots, he thought it only fair that that information be shared with his mother.

"I related only part of the conversation I had with Lex Stedman and Bruno Trosconi," the Chameleon confessed. "It is only fitting that I reveal the full conversation."

"Whatever are you talking about, Chris?" his mother asked. "Is there something important you failed to tell me?"

"Sadly enough, there is. During Trosconi's background check on the Iceman, he found some employment records in the archives of the State of New York."

"And . . ." his mother said as her eyes narrowed and she stared at her son.

"Guess who he was employed by at the time of Dad's death?"

"Chris, this is not fair . . ."

Before his mother could finish her statement, the Chameleon blurted, "Carleono."

"He was employed by Meloni's father?" she asked raising her eyebrows.

"By Baranetti's Sport Bar & Grill that was owned by Carleono."

Still with her eyebrows arched, she said, "So?"

"You need to hear the rest of it. At the time Dad was killed by the Iceman, Dad was investigating Carleono and his club concerning alleged payoffs to the NYPD."

His mother blanched.

"Yes! And, remember me telling you about the Iceman's DOJ reference and Lex telling me that the DOJ was a tribunal that was conceived and presided over by a law school dropout?"

"Of course, but . . ."

"Don't you get it? Carleono was a law school dropout and he and his uncle were involved in arbitration and mediation just like the tribunal. In other words, the DOJ was Carleono's brainchild."

The Chameleon's mother just closed her eyes and shook her head.

Both were silent for several long moments, and his mother, now with both hands to the sides of her head, broke the ice by declaring, "I can't believe Meloni's father had anything to do with your father's death. Hopefully, you don't think so either. That's a grand leap to surmise that her father must have been responsible merely because he was the owner of a club that was being investigated by the authorities and the person who allegedly killed your father was employed there."

"What about the law school connection?" The Chameleon's voice rose and he began to pace.

"A lot of people flunk or drop out of law school and for various reasons. Just because Carleono did doesn't mean that he was the Grand Wizard of the DOJ!"

"You don't doubt that the Iceman killed Dad, do you?"

"How do you know for sure? People confess to committing crimes they never committed all the time. What proof do you have that the Iceman was telling the truth? Besides, he never said Carleono ordered it."

"You would think someone who was about to die would tell the truth. I don't see what he would have to gain by admitting to a mortal sin he didn't commit."

"Let me be the Devil's Advocate for the moment. If the Iceman was in the condition you described," the Chameleon's mother added, "he no doubt was heavily medicated and receiving morphine. He might have been hallucinating and unaware of what he was saying. Your father used a name for that type of evidence."

"It would be incompetent evidence and deemed unreliable and inadmissible in a court of law, and you're correct," the Chameleon responded. "Other than the employment and law school connections, which I consider significant, we have no corroborating evidence."

"Even if the Iceman killed your father, it doesn't follow that Meloni's father ordered the hit. And, why wasn't Lex killed as well?"

"That's an easy answer. Lex abandoned the investigation. Dad didn't. It was Dad who was meeting with the informant stock broker and building a case against Carleono, not Lex. The fact that both Dad and the informant were killed is a pretty clear indication, at least to me, that Carleono was somehow involved."

"If the case against Carleono is so persuasive, why isn't the FBI clamoring to file murder charges? Wouldn't that be first degree murder?"

"If Carleono ordered it, he would be deemed to have been an accomplice or accessory to murder in the first degree and just as culpable as the Iceman. In answer to your first question, the quantity and quality of the evidence is not enough to charge Carleono, let alone convict him."

"I'm sorry. I'm not persuaded Carleono had your father killed. If he bought off the authorities and had them in his hip pocket, so to speak, then why would he resort to murder?"

"Dad could expose him. He definitely was an enemy of Carleono and of the mobsters, and the DOJ reputedly was dedicated to the extinction of the infidels."

"The Iceman put the blame of your father's death on the DOJ. What evidence do the authorities have that Carleono was involved in any way with the DOJ?"

"Only the law school connection, Mom, only the law school connection. However, in my mind that is significant and more than just a coincidence. Believe me, I hope I am wrong."

The Chameleon's discussion with his mother did little to resolve the issue of who ordered his father's execution. He felt like a ping-pong ball, going from one side and then to the other. He was more confused now than he was before and if the matter went to court and he were a juror in the case of *State versus Carleono,* he would have to admit that he had reasonable doubt and would have no choice but to vote for an acquittal.

The innocence or guilt of Carleono was something that would need to be placed on the back burner at least for now. The Chameleon had something more important to discuss with his mother. He had always been dependent upon his mother for advice and certainly on the matter he was about to discuss. It was now the most important thing in his life.

From his pocket, the Chameleon retrieved a fancy ring box. From inside, he carefully removed a diamond engagement ring that had to be at least two carats.

"For Meloni?" Adriana asked.

He handed the ring to his mother. "What do you think?"

She examined the ring and slipped it on her little finger. "Chris, I could not love you more. If I had a daughter, I could not love her any more than Meloni. If you should be so fortunate as to receive a yes for an answer, then I would insist that you change the priorities in your life and make her your number one. Otherwise, I think you should return the ring and get your money back."

"Do you think she will accept?" the Chameleon asked anxiously.

"Knowing your track record, I'd say no. However, if you make the changes you told me about, I'd say you have an outside chance."

Holding the Chameleon and holding him like only a mother could, she said, "Your love for

The CHAMELEON

Meloni and her love for you should be independent of everything else, and I mean everything else!"

The Chameleon knew what she meant. He also knew he could not give up the search for the Dispenser of Justice, whoever or whatever that might be, so that he could dispense his own brand of justice. He was convinced that he could do so without compromising his relationship with Meloni. At least, that was his hope. He may have been wrong, but he was not in doubt.

CHAPTER FOURTEEN

T he tragic death of the Chameleon's father was difficult for everyone, especially for the Chameleon. Because of his assuming the father's role for his younger brothers, he had little time to grieve. His anguish was constant but he felt he had to be strong not merely for his brothers but his mother as well. The risk that the whole family was in jeopardy dictated extreme measures that would alter their lives forever.

Assuming a new identity had presented its own brand of problems, not just logistically but emotionally as well. He was able to replace the initials on his luggage and nametags on his clothing but parting with much of his early life memorabilia was like erasing everything he held sacred. With an assumed name, he felt like an imposter. Yet, he understood that it was the key to the family's survival. He understood the concept of witness protection and that survival required fraud and deceit.

As the oldest, the Chameleon was proud of the family name. The Mira legacy had been handed down throughout the generations and the Chameleon had relished in listening to his father relate the legends his father had learned from the Chameleon's grandfather and great grandfather. The old Mira family scrapbooks would have to be left behind along with the family's true identity. That was the way it had to be.

New birth certificates and new Social Security numbers were issued and henceforth and forevermore thirty-one-year-old Adriana Mira would become Adriana Carcelli; seven-year-old Donato Leonardo Mira, Jr. would become Christopher Claudio Carcelli; five-year-old Francesco Alessandro Mira would become Frances Alexander Carcelli; and, three-year-old Antonio Giorgio Mira would become Anthony George Carcelli. The two younger brothers were not troubled by the name changes and, in fact, were enamored with the modern adaptation of their first and middle names.

When the Chameleon, together with Meloni and his mother, arrived at Miami International Airport that tropical December Friday, they were met by Frances and his wife of twenty-six years, Helena. Two years younger than the Chameleon, Franc looked like he was by far the older of the two brothers. With his chalk-white hair and mustache and his diminutive frame, he might have been mistaken for the Chameleon's father. His demeanor and appearance, however, were consistent with his title as a president of a prestigious bank in downtown Coral Gables.

The Chameleon towered over Franc as the two embraced.

"You haven't changed a bit," Franc said as they stood with their arms around each other. "In fact, you look better than I've ever seen you."

"Are you saying that I've not always been this good looking?" the Chameleon responded with his arms still wrapped around his brother's shoulders.

"Conceit still runs deep, I see."

The CHAMELEON

"My humility is exceeded only by my brilliance. And, you my dear brother look more like a supreme court justice than a banker."

"You have always been the son with the brawn. I've always been the one with the brains."

"Don't I get the credit here?" Adriana asked as both Franc and the Chameleon gathered her to them. The gush of tears from the three bespoke of the tenderness and love they shared.

Helena introduced herself to Meloni. "Looks like they've forgotten us. Let's remind them that we're here." The circle of intimates now grew to five.

Amidst tears of joy, cajoling and reminiscing, they headed for the baggage area.

When they entered the baggage area, the Chameleon spotted what looked like Charlie's Angels lying in ambush.

"Daddy! Daddy!" Caitlin and Chelsea screamed as they ran into the waiting arms of their father. "Uncle Chris," Lisha said as she too was soon part of the armful.

"How's university life?" the Chameleon asked Caitlin and Lisha, both of whom were attending the University of Miami in Coral Gables.

"I love it," Caitlin said with a broad grin.

"She loves it because of the boys," Lisha interrupted.

"Look who's talking," Caitlin said in a taunting voice.

"Now, now girls," Adriana scolded. "Your father has someone he wants you to meet."

"This is Meloni," the Chameleon said as he placed his arm around her.

To Meloni, he said, "These are my daughters, Caitlin and Chelsea, and my niece, Lisha."

As they shook hands with one another, the Chameleon said, "Caitlin is now nineteen and attends the University of Miami along with Lisha. Chelsea, this past month turned seventeen and will be a senior at Kennedy High School in Cincinnati next year."

"I've never seen three more attractive young women," Meloni commented as she smiled at the three. "And, you each look like models." The three blushed and grinned.

"Meloni owns a very fashionable ladies' clothing store in Chicago," Adriana said. "The compliment you just received is from an expert."

"What is the name of your store?" Chelsea eagerly asked.

"Magnelli's Boutique," Meloni responded.

"Is it on Michigan Avenue?" Caitlin asked.

"Are you familiar with my boutique?"

Caitlin grinned. "My mother took Chelsea and me there one time when we were visiting Daddy. In fact, we each bought a swimming suit there."

"My, what a small world!" Adriana exclaimed. "Weren't those the turquoise ones you wore one summer when we went up to Highland Park?"

"Yes, I believe they were," Caitlin replied.

"I remember those," Chelsea said excitedly. "It's too bad we outgrew them."

"If the three of you will give me your sizes before I leave, I will see that each of you receives the latest edition."

The three yelled an enthusiastic "Yeah!" and high-fived Meloni. Meloni had become an instant celebrity.

The carousel was now turning, laden with the bags from their flight. As their luggage was spotted, the Chameleon retrieved them. When he grabbed Adriana's bag, one of the handles broke. Caitlin whispered to Chelsea, "I know what we can get Grams for Christmas."

Caitlin and Chelsea had never seen their father with another woman, let alone one as stunning as Meloni. Since their parents divorced four years before, they had envisioned a day when the family would be reunited. Until now, reconciliation seemed a possibility, as both of their parents had remained unattached. Although they had been informed their father had someone special he wanted them to meet, they were totally unprepared for the moment.

"You're Dad's girlfriend?" Chelsea asked Meloni shortly after their introduction.

"You might call me that," Meloni said.

"I can see why Dad likes you," Caitlin added. "It's been a long time since I've seen him so happy."

"The feeling is mutual," Meloni responded.

"Have you and Uncle Chris known each other very long?" Lisha asked.

The Chameleon was out of earshot but could only imagine the uneasiness Meloni was

The CHAMELEON

feeling. He had been worried about how his daughters would react upon being introduced to the new woman in his life. He had dated little since the divorce and this would be the first time he would be accompanied to a family holiday gathering without Sandy being present. Even at Caitlin's high school graduation, he and Sandy had sat together and appeared as a couple.

When Adriana, who was standing with the girls, turned and winked at him, the Chameleon knew everything was going to be all right. As Adriana caught up to the Chameleon and slipped her arm through his, she whispered, "Guess who has captured the attention of your daughters?" The Chameleon was relieved. His daughters were more precious than gold. So was his mother. And Meloni? *That goes without saying,* he told himself. He would count and not compare his blessings this holiday season.

The homes lining the street leading to the Carcelli's Florida bungalow were innocuous enough. However, the humble outside of the

Carcelli residence proved to be deceptive, as Meloni would soon discover. It was not quite as impressive as Cousin Sal's or her father's home, but impressive nonetheless. It was spacious and comfortable. They had left Chicago to avoid the winter chill, and now were seeking respite from the soggy Miami heat. Walking into the air conditioned interior was a relief.

Meloni was barely in the door when a family portrait sitting on the top of an antique organ caught her eye. She surmised it was a photograph of the Chameleon's parents with their three sons. Adriana looked to be in her late twenties or early thirties. She recognized the tallest of the three boys as the Chameleon, who looked to be seven or eight at the time. The smallest was probably Tony, who looked to be about three or four, and the middle child was undoubtedly Franc, who she guessed to be five or six when the picture was taken. Her eyes, however, narrowed and became transfixed on the eyes of the adult male who was standing with Adriana in the center of the photograph. Those were piercing familiar eyes, and unquestionably the same eyes as the man she loved.

While the Chameleon was engaged in bringing in the luggage and unloading the Christmas gifts, Franc, noticing Meloni's preoccupation with the family portrait, set down his mother's baggage.

"That was the last picture the family took while my father was still alive," Franc said.

Even though the Chameleon was in his fifties, she was still intrigued by the uncanny likeness of him and his father. Meloni commented, "I grew up in New York City. Was that photograph taken on the steps of St. Patrick's Cathedral?"

"Yes!" Franc responded. "Three months later, our father was killed."

"What was your father's occupation?" Meloni asked.

"Didn't Chris tell you? He was an FBI agent killed in the line of duty. We were living in New York City at the time."

"Meloni!" she turned around to see the Chameleon holding her bags. "I'll put these in your room. Want to help?"

"Sure." She walked toward him, her mind preoccupied with what she'd just learned about his father.

The photograph had made his father come alive and she was haunted by the revelation that his father had been an FBI agent and had, while in the line of duty, met a violent death, leaving a widow and three fatherless children.

The empathy she was feeling for the family was tugging at her heart, as was the fact that the Chameleon had chosen, for whatever reason, not to share the intimate details surrounding the death of his father. It seemed odd. She wanted the two of them to be able to share everything. Wasn't she deserving of the revelation? She was troubled by what seemed like a cloak of secrecy. Being shut out was a rejection of sorts, and she was uncertain as to how to interpret his having withheld such vital information from her. She wondered what else he might be keeping from her.

Christmas Eve in Coral Gables was quite a contrast from the previous Christmas Eve spent in Chicago. And, it was not just the tropical weather and lack of snow that made this year so different. Being with his daughters was singularly exceptional but with the anticipated marriage proposal to Meloni his happiness grew exponentially.

Traveling down Ponce De Leon Boulevard, the Chameleon sensed Meloni was somewhat withdrawn and more reserved than usual. Perhaps it was his imagination and nervousness over making a commitment, knowing that this time it would have to be honored. That he loved Meloni with all his mind, heart and soul was indisputable. But would making her the center of his universe be a promise he could keep?

As they were nearing the Church of the Little Flower, the Chameleon checked his suit coat pocket to make sure the box containing Meloni's Christmas gift was still there. Perhaps he should remove the ring now to have it ready. But, then again, he didn't want to risk the chance that it might slip through the seams. He knew he could work it out of the box with one hand at the proper moment without risking detection. So, he eagerly waited.

Midnight mass was much more crowded than he had anticipated, especially in light of their early arrival. Although, they could not all be seated in one row, the five adults sat together directly behind the Chameleon's niece and two daughters. As the congregation concluded "Silent Night," the Chameleon reached across Meloni and, taking her left hand in his, slipped the sparkling diamond onto her ring finger and with tears in his eyes he whispered, "I love you. Will you marry me?"

Trembling with surprise and excitement and fighting to hold back tears of her own, Meloni offered her lips to him as an expression of unequivocal acceptance. With the deal sealed, the two stood in silent embrace as the celebrant gave the Christmas blessing and the choir began singing "Joy to the World."

CHAPTER FIFTEEN

It was traditional in the Carcelli household that they wait until Christmas morning to inspect Santa's nocturnal magic and open Christmas gifts. With the three teens, the Christmas observance was frenzy. The Chameleon watched with delight as the three tore open each gift and especially those that Meloni had helped select. Santa had been particularly solicitous of Adriana and the Chameleon shared his mother's joy as her eyes beamed with child-like excitement, since most of her gifts bore a Magnelli's Boutique sticker!

The Chameleon had saved his gift from Meloni until last. It appeared to be a Christmas card with season passes for one of Chicago's professional sports teams. However, the envelope was slightly heavier than he'd expected. Using the blade of his pocket knife, he sliced open the top. As the card with the manger scene was extracted, a small sealed manila envelope fell to the floor with a jingle—but not the jingle of bells. Without reading the card, he hastily ripped open the small envelope. Inside he found two keys fastened together and a folded catalog depiction of a shiny new ultra classic Harley-Davidson motorcycle and the business card of a salesman from a Chicago dealership.

As the contents of the smaller envelope were passed around, there were a lot of oohs and ahhs. "How fortunate he is to have a fiancé like Meloni," he heard Franc say to Helena. During the whole time, the Chameleon sat cross-legged in stunned silence. Although he tried, he could say nothing. There were no words to express his gratitude to God for having put Meloni in his life. If it were not for her, he would still be a lost soul. As she wrapped her arms around the Chameleon's neck, the glint of her engagement ring escaped the eyes of no one and symbolized the bright future that appeared to be in store for the two of them.

The CHAMELEON

Meloni's parents were scheduled to celebrate Christmas with Carleono's brother, Giovanni, and his wife, Sylvie, in the Bahamas. Eager to see their daughter and to spend more time with the Chameleon and his family, they had arranged to fly into the Miami area. Even though Franc and Helena had extended their hospitality to Carleono and Magdalena, the latter booked rooms at the Palacio de Esplendor in Miami Beach.

Having traveled across the southernmost causeway connecting Miami Beach to the mainland, with the adults in one vehicle and the teens in the other, Meloni and the Carcellis traveled down Hotel Row to rendezvous with Meloni's parents. Palacio de Esplendor was as its name implied. Situated on a diamond-white beach facing the Atlantic, they would have their white Christmas after all.

Eager to take advantage of that tropical Christmas day, little time was spent indoors and all opted to postpone lunch until they sufficiently sampled the alluring waves that licked the white grains of sand along Miami Beach.

Preparing to take advantage of the sun's rays and a dip into the Atlantic, the Chameleon removed the Miami Dolphins T-shirt he had received from Caitlin earlier that morning, thus exposing his St. Christopher medal and chain. He could see Carleono's eyes narrow and mouth open as Carleono stared at the medal.

"I've been admiring your medal, Christopher," Carleono said. "I never noticed it before. It's rather unique and appears to be an heirloom. Aren't you afraid it will be lost in the waves?"

"Actually, it's been in the family for several generations now. It was given to my father by his father and my mother gave it to me when I graduated from the police academy. I haven't removed it often since my mother first fastened it around my neck. Fortunately, the chain is fairly rugged and can't be slipped off without unfastening it."

"Do you mind?" Carleono asked as he touched the St. Christopher medal.

The Chameleon could almost hear Carleono's heart beat as the man gazed at the front and then the reverse side of the medal. Neither said anything for several long seconds.

The Chameleon was thinking that Carleono had connected the dots and had come to the stark realization that his beloved and only daughter was engaged to the son of the man whose execution he had ordered. What kind of havoc that must have been creating in Carleono's mind was something the Chameleon could only imagine. The Chameleon did know, however, that the finger of guilt was pointed squarely in Carleono's direction.

The Chameleon had been deliberately evasive about his immediate family history, both on this occasion as well as in the past. He had been very careful not to reveal to anyone his father's occupation, the circumstances of his death, the family's true identity or the family connection to New York City. Maybe this is the reason his undercover work had been so successful. He was able to improvise and mask deception with convincing clarity. Today it would be he who unveiled the skeletons that were locked in the closets of the past—not his, but Carleono's. At the time, the Chameleon was not aware of his brother's conversation with Meloni as she examined the family portrait upon her arrival.

CHAPTER SIXTEEN

I t was not difficult to convince Adriana that she should extend her stay in Florida. Following the weather report of the freezing temperatures in Chicago, the pleading of her granddaughters and the encouragement of the rest of the family, her decision was predictable. That meant Meloni and the Chameleon would be making the journey back home alone.

When Meloni rescheduled Adriana's flight, Meloni also finessed the exchange of cabin class for first-class seating.

"Now, I won't have to listen to your complaining and childish display of indignation," she said upon the Chameleon's discovery of the upgrade.

He gave her a puzzled look.

She laughed. "I could read your mind."

The plane had barely taken off when she looped her arm through his and gave him a strange look.

"Hey, why are you looking at me like that?" he asked. "I thought you loved me."

"I could not love you more. That's why I hope you won't mind if I ask you something that has been weighing on my mind and that has kept me awake for the past several nights."

With that she placed both of his hands in hers and squeezed. He could sense her desperation. She looked into his eyes and began to speak.

"When we first met, you said a lasting and meaningful relationship could only thrive on trust and confidence. As I recall, you said the relationship required transparency. You promised there would be no secrets and there would be no role playing."

The Chameleon detected a fragileness he'd never noticed before. Under the façade of a tough business woman was a vulnerability that he had recognized only in himself. Now, it appeared she was bearing her soul and pleading for reciprocity. If ever there was a time for him to be totally candid and yielding to Meloni, it was now.

Softly brushing away her tears with his fingers and kissing her gently on the lips, the Chameleon made a life-altering decision. He would tell her everything.

"Do you think I have been playing games with you?" he asked.

"My independence has become somewhat suspect since meeting you, Chris. I am appalled at how pliable I am, like putty in your hands."

He took a deep breath. "My real name is not Christopher or even Christopher Claudio Carcelli. That is an identity I assumed upon the death of my father in 1965. It is a long story and one that apparently needs to be told, at least to you. To even infer that you are like putty in my hands is the furthest thing from the truth. I wish it were true. In reality, you are the sculptor and I am the clay. By telling you of my past, my family and I are literally placing our lives in your hands. Now that we are engaged, you have earned the right to know and there is nothing I would or should ever keep from you. I love you more than myself or anyone or anything. I love you more than life itself."

Meloni was starting to have second thoughts. Maybe there were things that needed to go unsaid, at least for the time being. Perhaps she was being precipitous in her probing and he would think she was meddling. Regardless, she did not want to wound the love of her life. Nothing was worth the gamble.

"Chris, I trust you with my heart and soul. There is nothing that could change that. What you tell me or don't tell has absolutely no bearing upon my love for you. Clearly, I have crossed the bounds of decency in my desire to know everything about you. I apologize for what you might see as an invasion of your privacy. I didn't intend our conversation to be an inquisition. But you tell me what you need to tell me in your own way and in your own time."

He started to speak. Meloni pressed her right index finger against his lips and said, "Shhhh! You do not have to tell a story to stay alive."

In light of the reprieve and the anticipated quandary in which the Chameleon would be placed by revealing or not revealing his suspicion of her father's involvement in his father's death, the Chameleon welcomed Meloni's invitation of silence. It was a relief to the Chameleon and an opportunity to reconsider. If he spoke about his suspicions, he would risk antagonizing Meloni. By not revealing his deep-seated guilty hypothesis, he would be misleading her and she would feel deceived. In any event, he for the moment at least, had passed through the eye of the storm, emerging virtually unscathed. Revelations of the past could await another day.

The first order of business upon returning to Chicago was to stop at Kiddler's Motorcycles, Accessories and Supplies. There Meloni helped the Chameleon claim and inspect the limited production model of his Harley-Davidson Ultra-Classic Christmas gift. He knew and appreciated a good machine. Early in his career his love of bikes allowed him to penetrate a notorious motorcycle gang in Los Angeles while on loan to the LAPD. The only thing he had lacked in his disguise was the permanent tattooing. Otherwise, he was a convincing gang member and one of them.

Kiddler smiled expansively as the Chameleon straddled the hog in the showroom. "I can keep it in the back until you want to transport it," he offered.

"Not a chance," the Chameleon said with a laugh. "I'm taking this baby home right now."

Meloni protested. "The roads are too slick for a motorcycle. Why don't you leave it here?"

The look he gave her silenced her. "You can follow me in the car. If I crash and burn, you can pick up the pieces." With that he turned the key and punched the starter. The engine roared to life and he nodded to the salesman to open the door. In less time than it took Meloni to get her car keys out of her purse, he was out of sight.

When she arrived at the apartment, he opened the door and ushered her in.

"You have got to be kidding me!" she exclaimed as she saw the shiny green-and-chrome bike sitting in the middle of his living room, surrounded by furniture that had exceeded its life expectancy. It stuck out like a wart on the nose of a Hollywood starlet.

"It's a beauty," he said, ignoring her criticism. He took her in his arms and whirled her around. "As are you, love of my life."

"I'm certainly not going to burst your bubble," she replied, "but you might consider renting a garage."

"It's going to stay right here." He gave her a longing look. "How about you?"

"Nice try" she said. "But I need to get to the store and start inventorying stock. See you tomorrow?"

"Absolutely." He kissed her deeply, hoping to change her mind, but with a smile and a wave, she was gone.

As he went through the saddlebags, he was surprised to find the discarded sales tag wedged in the bottom of one. It bore the figure $36,500. He whistled in surprise, but only because he considered it such a bargain.

The Chameleon was beginning to wonder if his mother would be wintering in Miami when she rescheduled her return to Chicago until after the first of the year. Although he missed her, he was pleased that she was enjoying the breath of spring and spending time with the Florida Carcellis as well as his future in-laws. Actually, with regard to the latter, he was somewhat skeptical, not knowing what the future might bring.

The Chameleon was gripped with guilt whenever he was with his bride to be. His incessant preoccupation with Carleono's possible involvement in the death of his father was a constant companion, one that was making him oblivious to everything else. His compulsion to bring Carleono to justice was growing by the day and was twisting his thinking, especially when it came to Meloni. Subconsciously, he was beginning to blame her for the sins of her father. For that reason, their relationship had become somewhat shaky and was spiraling, but not necessarily upward.

It was at Sal's New Year's party that Meloni first suggested that the two start taking baby steps and not leap headlong into a sea of discontent. The Chameleon, from the time the two had met, had been mesmerized by Meloni.

The CHAMELEON

Although he at first recoiled at her suggestion and acted somewhat nonchalant, inside he was a bundle of nerves and in his mind he conjured up a number of unacceptable and distressing scenarios. To lose Meloni would be to lose everything. This would not be the time to become recalcitrant. Discretion was the better part of valor. To vacillate would be the kiss of death. Yet, he was driven by an inexplicable compulsion to do just the opposite.

Fortunately, their flayed feelings were short lived and 2008 was harkened in with the gusto expected of the newly engaged.

"Happy New Year, Superman," Meloni whispered into the Chameleon's ear as the band heralded in the new year. "I can hardly wait to spend the rest of my life with you."

"Hey, how long can you two do that without taking a breath?" Sal asked while Meloni and the Chameleon kissed and held each other close.

When they did not respond, Lenna said, "Shall we pin a do not disturb sign on your backs?"

"Very funny," Meloni said as she and the Chameleon responded to the interruption. "You're obstructing progress."

The Chameleon was already formulating his list of New Year's resolutions. Bringing the architect of his father's death to justice was still at the fore of his list. He, perhaps foolishly, believed that was compatible with and not detrimental to the second on his list: developing a lasting relationship with Meloni.

CHAPTER SEVENTEEN

I t had been less than a month since Meloni's engagement to the Chameleon and her return trip from Florida. Now, she found herself on a flight to Lake Tahoe responding to a distress call from her father concerning her mother's deteriorating cardiac condition. At the Chameleon's urging, she was on her way to be at her mother's side.

Meloni had slept little the night before and remembered Adriana having motioned to her to accompany her to the lady's room during their dinner at Bernarde's. "I don't mean to meddle," she had said in their privacy, "but I sense some tension between you and Chris. Is there anything I can do to help? You know, I love you both."

Meloni now felt embarrassed recalling how she had to be consoled by Adriana as she sobbed. "I love your son and I love you, too," she remembered telling Adriana. Now, she wasn't sure how much her anxiety over concern for her mother's health played in her distress but she was sure her distress over her relationship with Chris was almost too much to bear. Though she did not relish the thought of being away from Chris, she thought the hiatus might not be such a bad thing.

Although not quite Florida weather, Martin Luther King, Jr. Day at Lake Tahoe was a respite from the harsh Chicago temperatures and storms that had been whipping the eastern half of the United States the past several days. Meloni was met at the airport by both her father and mother who had returned home to Tahoe. Magdalena's chest pains had subsided and she was faring well with the prescribed medication. Magdalena did not look any worse for wear. For that Meloni was both grateful and relieved.

Upon reaching South Shore, and being ushered to her private quarters in the company of her mother, Meloni was unable to mask the consternation and frustration that had been festering since her Christmas trip to Coral Gables.

"What's wrong, child?" Magdalena asked as tears rolled down Meloni's cheeks.

Meloni could not speak but buried her head in her hands and sat on the edge of the bed.

"Here, take this," Magdalena said as she handed Meloni a fistful of tissues and, sitting next to Meloni, placed her arms around her.

As Meloni's sobs subsided somewhat, Magdalena asked, "Is it Chris?" More sobs.

Magdalena attempted to console Meloni. "Nothing is ever as bad as it seems."

"You don't know about our situation," Meloni managed to say. "Chris is everything I ever wanted."

After long moments, Magdalena said, "Try to dry up the tears. Your father is anxious to visit with you."

Neither said anything as they ambled arm in arm down the winding corridor leading to the smallest of the patios overlooking the lake. Seated at the exquisitely decorated table, sipping on an extra-dry martini with the obligatory oversized green olive, was Carleono. His expression changed upon witnessing Meloni's distress. He rose to embrace and comfort his daughter, whose teardrops again began to flow. The three poured out what they later laughingly referred to as buckets. Derrik, the Baranetti's longtime butler, waited until the emotion subsided before bringing refreshments all around.

"I hope your mother's health is not the cause of your misery," Carleono said as he sat down.

"Naturally, I was worried about Mom," Meloni responded as she blinked back tears.

"I have had a lot on my plate lately and seeing the two of you has made me more emotional than normal. I have missed you both so much!" With that, Meloni let go of her mother's hand and went to sit beside her father.

"I didn't want to alarm you," Carleono said. "We didn't know how serious the chest pains were this time and knew you would want to be here. Besides, we have some important matters to discuss with you." When Meloni looked at one and then the other with an expression of grave concern, Carleono said, "No, it's not what you think. It's not about your mother's or my health. It is about your future wedding plans."

"You needn't worry," Meloni responded. "We've put everything on hold. I am puzzled and don't know what to do. Something is troubling Chris and he is unable to confide in me. I love him dearly and I know he loves me as well. However, of late he has been erecting a wall between us and steering me away from him."

"Your father and I both care for Chris but your father has some concerns," Magdalena said. "He may be seeing ghosts. Ever since Christmas Day your father has been troubled. Maybe it is better that I let him explain."

Taking the last sip of his martini, Carleono began. "Christmas Day was the first time I took particular note of Chris' medal and chain. Both are rather intriguing, not only because of their bulk but because of their unique craftsmanship and certainly their antiquity. Chris claims it was his father's and was given to him by his mother upon his graduation from the police academy."

Directing his question to Meloni he asked, "Do you know anything about Chris' father?"

"According to his brother, Franc, his father was an FBI agent stationed in New York

City and was killed in the line of duty sometime in 1965."

Carleono's face became ashen. "I thought so," he said. "I thought so." He closed his eyes and shook his head.

Meloni put her hand on his arm. "Why do you ask?"

Momentarily, Carleono was at a loss for words. Tracing the curve of the martini glass with his right index finger, he blurted, "I have something that I've told no one, not even your mother until recently. I must have your pledge that you will tell no one, not even Chris— *especially* not Chris. Do I have your word?"

"Of course." She frowned at her father.

"Let me emphasize the sacredness and the importance of your promise. Should the information I am about to reveal reach the wrong ears, not only my safety but yours as well could be in jeopardy. I hesitate, not because I am afraid you will make disclosure. I know you won't. However, I compromise your wellbeing by those who will stop at nothing to elicit such information by any means, and I mean *any* means."

The CHAMELEON

"Daddy," Meloni hastily interrupted. "No one will ever know you told me and I am not afraid." With that she smiled at her beloved father.

He continued, "Being successful in the business world, particularly the type of business I inherited from my Uncle Nick, required me taking shortcuts and risks. Some of those shortcuts and risks, if not illegal, were in some ways unethical. Gambling and prostitution in New York were clearly outlawed in those days, as they are today. However, they were never considered mortal sins. They would have gone on whether my Uncle Nick was involved or not. Controlling gambling and prostitution the way we did really harmed no one, and like my Uncle Nick, I considered that we were performing a public service. I never considered what we were doing dishonest. Plus, everything I did was a win-win proposition. The sums I may have cheated Uncle Sam out of I repaid ten-fold by my charitable contributions and community involvement. Perhaps I rationalized my way to accumulating wealth. However, I don't see any difference between what I am doing in the state of Nevada where gambling is legal and what I or my uncle did in the state of New York where gambling was illegal. I'm not trying to validate what I did by telling about these things."

"Carley," Magdalena interrupted, "Your mercantile company and other businesses were legitimate, as are the family enterprises today. You make it sound as if our wealth was illegally gotten. It certainly wasn't and is the result mainly of good business judgment, sacrifice and hard work."

"Angel," Carleono responded. "You are absolutely correct. However, the self-flagellation was done as a prelude to what I am about to tell Meloni. She has always been told about the good but never the bad or the ugly. She deserves to hear it all. Otherwise she will not understand and will have only a distorted picture."

Meloni interrupted. "Daddy, I love and admire you. Nothing you or anyone could say would ever change that." Meloni sat on her father's lap and gave him a hug and kiss on the cheek, reminiscent of bygone days.

The emotional meeting was interrupted by Riccardi, who had served as the Baranettis' head chef for almost twenty-five years. "Lunch is ready when you are," he announced.

The CHAMELEON

"Wonderful!" Carleono said. "What's on the menu?"

Riccardi smiled. "Miss Meloni's favorite: Mahi piccata with Florentine rice and chocolate ganache cake for dessert."

"You remembered." Meloni gave the chef a quick hug as she passed him on her way to the dining room.

After lunch, the three retired to Carleono's private study. Meloni and her parents sat in red leather-chairs situated on three sides of an oversized glass coffee table. An ornate crystal tray containing a brandy decanter and three matching snifters sat on top of the table. The set was reputedly a prized possession of Warren G. Harding. Meloni had to chuckle as she looked around at the trappings of her father's study. The room where the tray with the fancy decanter and snifters had sat while the Hardings occupied the White House no doubt paled in comparison to the room where the Baranettis now sat. Carleono was not president of the United States but to Meloni, he was of equal or greater importance.

Upon closing the large wooden mahogany doors to the study, the staff was instructed that the three Baranettis were not to be disturbed.

There, Carleono, Magdalena and Meloni would spend the next several hours.

Still determined to tell all, Carleono began where he had left off. "Even though there is much that you already know, there is still much to tell."

"When my Uncle Nick first came to the United States in the early 1900s, he was only sixteen years of age and spoke little English. Being robust and at the same time street-smart, he was quickly integrated into New York's Italian community. Even as a young man, his counsel was highly sought and respected. He was a peace maker and resolved squabbles both within and among families. He was perceived as being fair and not on the take.

"It was my Uncle Nick who bankrolled my college education and insisted I go to law school. He wanted me to be a judge someday. He was very disappointed when I failed to take advantage of my law school opportunity. Having been involved in the family businesses, I was more interested in pursuing the various angles and generating an income than becoming a lawyer.

"After dropping out of law school, I was Uncle Nick's protégé. Despite my free spirit and lack of conformity with my parents' expectations, Uncle Nick still had faith in me. Probably everything I am and have is a result of Uncle Nick having taken me under his wings. By the time I was twenty-two, I was serving on arbitration panels with Uncle Nick, and eventuality was called upon to arbitrate complex and contentious disputes.

"Uncle Nick passed away in 1950. By then, I had been completely integrated into his businesses. As a mediator, he functioned on both sides of the law. Other than not having Uncle Nick at my side, everything proceeded as before. In fact, since I was not as conservative as Uncle Nick, the net worth of Baranetti Enterprises, Inc. went from a million to over a billion dollars.

"In mid-1964, the heads of two crime families came to me with a border dispute and asked me to intervene. I guess I would have been around forty at the time. By coincidence, I had attended grade school with both of them. Ezio Fredanado lived just down the street from me and had been one of my closest friends. Living down in the next block was a playmate and classmate of the two of us. His name was Evon Rigoletti. Evon was just a nickname. Everyone knew him as

Giovanni Rigoletti. Yes, the notorious mobster who later was convicted on tax evasion charges and who ultimately died in federal prison.

"Not only did Evon and Ezio agree to my proposed solution, but the two saw merit in the formation of a panel that would arbitrate differences between warring crime families. It was not very long before the panel became an active and efficient alternative to a duel at sunrise. All realized nothing would be accomplished by the pillage, burn and maim approach then being practiced by the warring factions on an indiscriminate basis.

"Little did I realize that by bringing the two together, I was creating a monster. The alliance that was formed between the two in the business world would probably be called a consolidation. To begin with, the three of us were able to reach a consensus. It was not long, however, before I became the lone dissenter or what you might call the odd man out. Evon became the ring leader and the two combined for some rather fanatic and erratic decisions. When they started planning the purging of perceived enemies, including government officials and law enforcement officers, I withdrew. I was replaced by Mongo Almandreo, the head of the largest and most powerful crime family then in New York.

"Almandreo and I had been on the outs ever since I became involved in Uncle Nick's nightclub. Pirating the opposition's help was a crime in the trade, especially back then. Whether it was showgirls, bartenders or bouncers, Almandreo used Baranetti's Sport Bar & Grill as his recruiting grounds. We prided ourselves on the caliber of our help, and Almandreo seized upon the opportunity to provide just the right incentives to lure them away. I often wondered if he hadn't used some strong arm tactics or extortion as part of his recruitment approach, as he always seemed to hire away our first-round draft picks.

"When I found out that one of my new hires was actually committing industrial espionage by passing on our trade secrets, he was immediately fired. Later we found out the man we knew as Gennaro Orazdenelli or simply as the General was an Almandreo plant who later went by the nickname Iceman. I tell you this because it has a bearing on the most important aspect of my exposition.

"It was the illegal gambling, and I am embarrassed to say, favors paid by our showgirls, that made the clubs prosper. The clubs, of course, were able to thrive under the noses of the authorities only as a result of their cooperation. The shakedown came from three of NYPD's finest, and believe it or not, a federal agent. The extortionists must have made quite a haul because, as I learned later, they received payola from virtually every club in the Bronx as well as neighboring boroughs."

Meloni sat in silence as she listened to her father. Her mother reached over and patted her hand.

Stopping only long enough to take a sip now and then from his martini, Carleono continued, "I know Evon and Ezio were assessed a king's ransom for their advanced raid warnings and pledges of silence because they as well as others shared that information with me. I assume Almandreo was a subscriber of their services as well, as he, too, was able to operate with impunity.

"I heard from underground sources that sometime in the winter of 1965 an FBI agent had been killed while conducting some kind of

surveillance at St. Sebastian's Catholic Church in
the Bronx. I was told that the hit was by the
General, later dubbed the Iceman, and that
Almandreo had in his possession a trophy that
had been provided by the Iceman as proof of a
successful hit. Later I saw a photograph of his so-
called trophy. It was a medal and chain that
appeared to be identical to the medal and chain
Chris wears. It was provided by Evon, who
bragged that Almandreo had an FBI agent on the
take, someone who kept him informed of the
authorities' every move. In fact, it was the FBI
insider who revealed that the dead agent had
incriminating evidence against the panel and
various clubs and club owners."

Meloni was stunned. Sorrow gripped her.
Captivated by the implications, all she could do
was sit in stony silence and shake her head.

"Your father thinks it was more than just
a coincidence that you and Chris met," Magdalena
finally said.

"What do you mean?" Meloni managed
to ask, still shaking her head in wonderment and
disbelief.

"Chris probably knows all the things your
father has just told you. Your father believes that

police intelligence has identified you on their radar screen as being the daughter of one of the members of the infamous panel that was connected to Chris's father's death. Maybe he thinks you can provide some of the pieces of the puzzle that have eluded law enforcement these last fifty years. That certainly would be something that would be on his mind and something that would account for his sudden preoccupation, especially since meeting your father."

"Are you saying Chris is using *me* to investigate Daddy?" Meloni asked, horrified. "That's absurd!"

"I'm only saying it's a possibility," Magdalena said apologetically.

Carleono had become unusually quiet and circumspect. He could see the impact Magdalena's words were having on their daughter. Magdalena's words were stinging but perhaps not as stinging as his might have been. Conceivably, he was overreacting and reading into the situation a conclusion that was unwarranted. For Meloni's sake he hoped so.

The CHAMELEON

Meloni was unable to sleep that night. She was tormented by the thought that her Prince Charming might not be the real thing, but in reality a cheap imitation, an imposter, and a fake. After all, he was an undercover agent, a professional master of disguise and master of deception by trade. Apparently, he was very good at what he did. If indeed it was all a charade, he certainly had performed it to perfection.

Meloni had an incessant urge to remove her engagement ring and discard it. Each time she started to slip it off her finger, she hesitated. In spite of her father's revelations, she couldn't picture the Chameleon as a conniving manipulator. She had found only love, loyalty and kindness in his arms. It was she who had turned away when he offered an explanation.

Yes, Chris had showed up out of nowhere. Yes, he appeared to be too good to be true. Yes, he withheld information relevant to their relationship. Yes, he seemed to be preoccupied by some unyielding and indefinable force. Yes, he lived a secret lifestyle. And, yes, his past was guarded. But, didn't he hint that all those things were inherent in the nature of the beast, the beast in his make-believe world as an undercover agent?

Meloni knew herself to be intuitive. She had never been made to feel that Chris's intentions were other than honorable. There were no warning signs or red flags to put her on notice that anything was amiss. He told her that there were some things that could not be revealed but would be someday. A mask of contrived love was not something he could wear very well without her detection. She not only believed him when he said she captured his deepest desires but she sensed it as well. Her parents had not exposed any charade; everything was pure supposition on their part. Now was not a time to be guided by emotion. However, her mind and heart were on a collision course. The true course she knew not. The one thing she was certain of was her profound confusion.

When the Chameleon called Meloni on her cellphone the following day, she hid her true feelings. She sounded upbeat and cheerful. When she hung up, she felt guilty for having dispensed her own brand of deception. She was still in the throes of sorting out her own true feelings and maybe hadn't been deceptive at all. If she was, the Chameleon hadn't detected it and she was too confused to objectively evaluate it. It was then she called on a greater power for guidance.

CHAPTER EIGHTEEN

While Meloni pondered the dubious future with the Chameleon, the Chameleon was preoccupied with solving the riddle to his father's death. With Meloni away, the quest to bring Carleono to justice was all-consuming. His malevolence towards Carleono gradually distorted his objectivity.

"Hello, Lex?" The Chameleon said.

"Speaking," Lex said.

"Hope I'm not bothering you. This is Chris Carcelli. I apologize for not calling earlier."

"I don't usually go to bed until quite late," Lex said. "Even if I were in bed, you wouldn't be bothering me in the least. What's on your mind?"

The CHAMELEON

"After all you have done for the family, I am embarrassed by having withheld some information from you that might have some bearing on fingering the source behind my father's execution."

Lex began to cough and managed a barely audible apology. "Continue," he finally said.

"When I spoke with you and Bruno Trosconi, you mentioned the name of Carleono Baranetti, the most likely suspect and crime figure connected to the death of my father."

"Yes," Lex responded. "You said you might know him."

"More than know him. What would you say if I told you I was engaged to his daughter?"

"Engaged to Carleono's daughter?" Lex said incredulously.

"I met Carleono's daughter purely by chance last July and proposed to her on Christmas Eve."

"Then you have no doubt met her father, the man who may very well be connected to your father's death? Correct?" Lex seemed anxious for a response.

"I have been with him on several occasions."

"Does he know your true identity?"

"He knows my affiliation with the CPD, and after observing my father's St. Christopher's medal around my neck, he no doubt has put two

220

and two together. His reaction was much the same as the Iceman's when he examined the medal and chain."

"So, he recognized it, did he? Did he say anything?"

"Just his look said it all."

"Why didn't you tell me this before?" Lex asked.

"I didn't want to be disloyal to his daughter."

"Do you . . . do you refer to Melonaya, who would be about forty-one?"

"Actually, she goes by the name of Meloni and she just turned forty in October. How did you know?"

"The FBI has had Carleono in their sights for a number of years, and I have been studying their reports and Bruno Trosconi's files. By the way, how close have you and Carleono become?"

"If you're asking if he told me anything connected to my father's execution or whether I have shared my family's history with him, the answer is no. I have been deliberately evasive with him as he has with me. I have not even shared my family history with Meloni."

"You do realize that blood is thicker than water. What you tell Meloni will ultimately reach her father's ears."

"And, what her father tells her will ultimately become pillow talk with me. Right?"

Lex was quiet for several long seconds. His silence was disquieting. He finally spoke.

"I don't suppose she has given you any hints about her family secrets that could provide us with any leads, has she?"

"Frankly, I would be very surprised if she knows anything. And, even if she did, I think it is way too early in our relationship for her to compromise her family loyalty."

"It's uncanny that the son of a slain FBI agent is engaged to the daughter of a crime figure who may very well be responsible for the execution order. Who sought whom out?"

"Actually, it was me who made the initial contact."

"If she had made the initial contact, then I would surmise that she was being used by her father to infiltrate law enforcement."

"You don't suppose her father, especially since he has put two and two together, now thinks that I made the contact with his daughter with the specific design of infiltrating him, do you?"

"That's a strong possibility. If she cools, then you will know her father is suspicious of your true intentions and no doubt has planted the seeds of doubt and discontent in her mind."

"You must have a crystal ball, Lex, because that is exactly what has happened. At least that explains her recent behavior. Ever since her father spied the medal around my neck, Meloni has become distant. And, it is not just my imagination. My mother has noticed it as well."

"Did you make reference to the St. Christopher medal originally belonging to your father?"

"Yes," the Chameleon replied.

"I take it Meloni has a close relationship with her father."

"She's an only child. She is very close to her parents, especially her father. Carleono would, without question, communicate his skepticisms and distrust of my motives to his daughter. He would probably do it for two reasons. The first would probably be to insulate her from what he would perceive to be deception and ultimate disappointment. The second would be to maintain his invincibility by avoiding exposure."

"Don't you think Meloni's father is also afraid that his daughter might reveal some of the family's deep, dark secrets to which she may have been exposed over the years?"

"As you yourself have said, Carleono has escaped the clutches of the law due to his cunning, caution and concealment. Certainly, he would have been careful not to have revealed information that might hurt his own well-being or that of his daughter."

"So far he has kept his mouth shut. But like the Iceman, there may come a day when he feels confession is good for the soul."

"Knowing Carleono, I think he will take all his secrets to the grave. The code of silence is one he considers sacred and one he will honor. I'm sure there are secrets he hasn't even shared with his wife, let alone his daughter."

"Let me ask you this, Chris, and this is critical. Has Carleono dropped any hints that might be helpful in the investigation of your father's death—other than his reaction upon seeing your father's St. Christopher medal?"

"Absolutely not, but then again I have spent very little time with him. As for his reaction to the medal, his curiosity might have been totally innocent and I might have read more into the incident than it warranted, although I don't think so."

"Has Carleono said anything that might have connected him to the tribunal we think he created?"

"Not one word. He did admit to flunking out of law school, but that is the closest thing he has come to confirming the FBI's suspicions."

"Has Carleono pumped you about your family background or about your father's occupation?"

"Unfortunately, my brother Franc told Meloni that our father had been an FBI agent and was killed in the line of duty. In a weak moment, I disclosed to Meloni that Carcelli was an assumed name. Meloni also noticed that an old family photograph had been taken on the steps of St. Patrick's Cathedral in New York City and, of course, she recognized the setting, having grown up in New York City herself."

"Do you know whether or not Meloni passed that information onto her father?"

"Right now she's at her parents' home at Lake Tahoe. Since we are now engaged, it would be natural for their discussion to center around our wedding plans, which no doubt include a discussion about me and my family. I would not be at all surprised if they compared notes and shared the information that has up to now remained confidential."

"I think you are correct in assuming this information will fall into Carleono's hands. What effect that will have upon the FBI's investigation and upon your relationship with Meloni I'm not sure. I do know Carleono will be more guarded. Forewarned is forearmed, as they say. Damage control in the Baranetti household may mean the return of your engagement ring."

Wild and crazy things raced through the Chameleon's head. He felt a sickness he had only felt once before in his half century on this planet. That was when he was seven years of age and lost another love in his life. To lose Meloni would be like losing his own life. He had survived the loss of his father but was uncertain whether he could survive the loss of Meloni.

"Are you there?" Lex asked anxiously.

"You hit me between the eyes," the Chameleon said. "The thought of Meloni returning the engagement ring is like receiving a death sentence. I guess I feel my world is crumbling around me."

"Things happen for the best. Trust in a greater power. It's better to find out now if the two of you are not suited for each other."

"I guess time will tell. Meloni will be returning to Chicago the day after tomorrow and we will know then or shortly thereafter what the future has in store for the two of us."

"Please call and let me know what happens. In the interim, the FBI, no doubt, will continue to pursue all leads and I will assist where I can."

"Lex, you were a friend of my father and now me. Our family can never thank you enough. How can we ever repay you?"

"The truth is I could never do enough. Until the architect of your father's death is brought to justice, I will not rest."

"None of us will." Unfortunately, the Chameleon didn't then realize the prophetic nature of his statement. If he had, he would have changed his current course of action. As it was, he was on a collision course with destiny.

CHAPTER NINETEEN

Tracy's Sports Bar was the watering hole for off-duty personnel of the CPD. It was Saturday night and Meloni was not due to return until late Sunday.

Seated at the bar with the Chameleon and sharing a pitcher of the house's ale were fellow detectives Sherwood Farrell and Geraldo Pastori. Their rumination over the department's austerity program and anemic support staff dominated their conversation despite the two tables of sorority girls on break behind them.

"You don't deserve a cost-of-living increase," Farrell said to the Chameleon. "The only overtime you're putting in is with Meloni."

"Don't pick on Chris," Pastori said. "Now that he is about to be a kept man, he doesn't need the city's damn money."

"Is that why I always get stuck with the bar tabs?" the Chameleon asked as he retrieved the pitcher and topped his mug.

Distracted by their intense mutual commiseration and his preoccupation with solving his father's murder and the quandary he was facing with Meloni, the Chameleon did not see the middle-aged woman station herself beside him. It was only when she ordered the tequila sunrise that he became aware of her.

When the Chameleon sized up the woman who introduced herself as Carmen, he saw a half-century old barfly, masquerading as a quarter-century cougar. As she gazed over at him and batted a cheap set of false eyelashes, he grimaced and took a gulp from his mug. He noted the flimsy top and short skirt, and concluded that the exposure of the body parts sadly betrayed her vintage, considering her attributes, or more aptly, the lack thereof.

She remained undaunted and shifted on her bar stool. "You're probably wondering why someone like me is out drinking in this dingy bar all alone," Carmen said, pouting as she looked at the Chameleon with sad eyes, framed by deep lines that indicated a life of hard living.

"Not really," the Chameleon replied. "Lots of ladies like to drink alone," he said gesturing with his chin toward a skinny, bleached blond woman staring into her glass at the other end of the bar.

"Well, I'm tired of being a lonely woman with a poor excuse for a husband."

"Marriage crumbling?" the Chameleon asked as he set down his mug.

"Has been for some time. My parents begged me not to marry Percy."

"I take it Percy is not the love of your life."

"You wouldn't want your sister or daughter to be married to Percy. He's the most controlling person I know. He treats me like a child and makes me account for every penny. I do get what I call an allowance, but he insists on knowing what I spend the money on. He even picks out my clothes. With him in the picture, I have no breathing room."

"Why did you marry him?"

Carmen pursed her lips and said, "He wasn't like that when I married him."

So you turned him into the despicable creature he is today? The question perched on the tip of his tongue, but he thought the better of it.

Carmen drank deeply and held the glass between her palms. "I'm sick of Percy and sick of married life. I want a change of scenery." She sniffed and the Chameleon thought she might cry, but she didn't.

Overhearing the conversation, Pastori nudged the Chameleon and prompted him to ask why she hadn't sought a divorce.

"Why haven't you filed for a divorce?" the Chameleon asked on cue.

"He vowed that if I ever left him it would be with the clothes on my back. He also said he would haunt me for the rest of my life. I'm afraid."

"Have you gone to the police? The laws in our state are designed to protect spouses who find themselves in your situation."

"You don't know Percy. He is very vindictive and doesn't make idle threats." She laughed bitterly. "I've got the bruises to prove it."

"Throw him out and get a restraining order. That's why there are enforcement and protection agencies."

She eyed him for a moment. "You sound like an attorney."

"I wish I were. If I was, I would be sitting in some fancy lounge watching classy entertainment and sipping Courvoisier instead of cheap beer."

She took the Chameleon by surprise when she asked, "You know of anyone who's not squeamish about performing a rather personal and sensitive mission?"

"You sound like you're looking for a hit man," he laughed, but knew she was serious.

Carmen cocked an eyebrow and stared at the Chameleon. "In my purse are five Gs for someone willing to eradicate a blight that has plagued me for the past thirty plus years."

"You don't really mean that."

"It needs to be done. You look like someone who wouldn't be afraid to do it," she responded still looking at him.

"How do you know that I'm not a cop"

"Because you look like crap. Besides, I just have a feeling you are the right person for the job."

Usually, it was the Chameleon who sought out the target. Suddenly it was the other way around. The first thing that came into the Chameleon's mind was that it was either a joke or a setup. In either case, he didn't want to be the goat.

He got up and threw some bills on the bar. "Tell me how and when I can get in touch with you."

"No way. I will contact you. Got a number?"

"Let's make it easy. How about I meet you back here at eight p.m. tomorrow night? Then, I won't be with company. Can you make it?"

"I can make it." She paused and drained her glass. "So, who are you?"

Glancing at the neon promo sign hanging at the back of the bar, the Chameleon responded, "Bud, just call me Bud."

After Carmen departed, the Chameleon put his hand to his head and murmured, "Oh my God!"

"I tried to play deaf and dumb," Pastori said. "What a nut case!"

"Damn! I promised to pick Meloni up at the airport tomorrow night."

"I'll do it for you," Pastori said. "Anything for a friend."

"Some friend! Are you suddenly conniving to steal another man's girl?"

"Totally honorable," Pastori said. He slapped the Chameleon on the back. "I don't know what it is about you, dude, but you are the only person I know who would have a murder-for-hire plot plopped into your lap."

The Chameloen frowned. "I have to follow this one and why you have to pick up Meloni. I'm doubtful Carmen would agree to a substitution."

Upon arriving back at his apartment, the Chameleon immediately telephoned Meloni.

"Still miss me?" Meloni asked sweetly as she answered her cell phone.

"Have you been gone?" the Chameleon asked.

"Very funny," Meloni scolded. "Remember you will be picking me up at the airport at seven forty-five tomorrow night. I will be the one with all the carry-ons."

"That's why I called. I . . . "

"Meloni interrupted. "Don't tell me you have a hot date and can't make it."

"Something unexpected came up. Work related," he added.

"In what role this time?"

"As a hit-man for hire."

"Be serious!"

"I *am*. This broad wants to off her husband."

"A divorce won't work?"

"Too slow and cumbersome."

"What's the going rate for the alternative to divorce?"

"Five Gs."

"Probably cheaper than a divorce, not to mention a lot more permanent!"

"Oh, honey, I'm sorry about this. I've arranged for Pastori to pick you up at the airport."

"Not necessary. Cousin Sal said he'd pick me up if you're unavailable."

The CHAMELEON

"See you sometime tomorrow night?"

"I won't hold my breath."

After hanging up the telephone, the Chameleon called Morton Weston, head of the detective squad.

"Sorry to bother you at home."

"You already have the weekend off."

"That's not why I called. Pastori and I have become involved in a murder-for-hire plot."

"Good thing I didn't go with the two of you to Tracy's tonight."

"How did you know it involved Tracy's?"

"Just hung up the phone with Pastori. He filled me in on the details."

"What do you think?"

"Solicitation, in itself, is a felony but we don't have enough at this point to charge let alone convict. What about wearing a wire?"

"Agree. I have no doubt that she will say everything we need to hear. She appears to like her booze and it seems it gets her in a real chatty mood."

"When she hands you the blood money, that's it. We'll have a surveillance van posted near the building. They'll record the conversation and make the bust as soon as she hands you the cash."

"I'll be at Tracy's around seven tomorrow night, a half-hour before Carmen is scheduled to arrive.

"Keep me posted!" Weston said as he hung up.

The Chameleon waited for Carmen at a corner table while sipping a beer. He looked at his watch as she walked through the door, her eyes scanning the room. "The time is eight-fourteen p.m.," he spoke lowly into the hidden recording device as his wire was activated. "Suspect has just entered Tracy's Sports Bar."

He made a slight gesture and she walked toward the table. He was startled by the difference in her attire from the night before. She could have passed as the local librarian. Carmen sat down across from him and declined his offer of a drink.

Instead she said, "Give me a club soda with a dash of Grenadine and wedge of lime."

The cocktail waitress leaned over the table as she wrote up the tab. The Chameleon marveled at how she managed to keep her ample breasts from escaping the scanty top that also exposed a slim midriff.

While Carmen waited for her drink, she pulled a folded envelope from her purse and handed it to the Chameleon. "Here is my earnest money—call it a deposit. I give you one thousand dollars now and the other four thousand when the job is done." She pulled out another envelope that held the rest of the money. She fanned through the bills with her thumb to assure him it was all there then stuffed it back into her purse.

The Chameleon marveled at her matter-of-fact demeanor as he counted the money in his envelope, careful not to obliterate any fingerprints, then pushed it into his shirt pocket. He easily shifted into his role as he had done many times before.

He leaned toward Carmen and spoke in a low tone as if to keep others from hearing. "Okay, since I'm the one taking all the risk here, I need to know everything about this guy so when the job is done, it doesn't look like a hit. Ya know what I mean? I also want to know when I get my money. I don't like working on 'deposits'."

"You'll get your money. My husband is Percy Ballard. He works at Hayden-Lenard

Distributing Company, just five blocks south of here on Potomac Boulevard. Are you familiar with Hayden-Lenard?"

"Bought a keg there a time or two." He chuckled then got back to business. "I need your husband's picture, a work schedule, where you live, all of that."

"Carmen pulled a photograph of Percy and herself from her billfold and ripping it in half, gave the Chameleon the half containing just Percy.

"I'd rather that nothing happen on our home turf. I don't want any fingers pointing at me."

"Yeah, well I need a Plan B, just in case. Things don't always go like they're supposed to."

"I prefer not to have it happen at the house. I may want to sell it, and nowadays, realtors have to disclose any previous 'issues'."

The Chameleon thought he had heard it all, but Carmen's callous attitude in the planning of the murder of a man to whom she had been married for over thirty years was something at which to marvel. She didn't want her husband's blood on her hands, figuratively speaking, but certainly not in actuality–especially if it soiled her nice neat home.

"Are you sure you want to go through with this? There is always time to change your mind. I don't want you whining with remorse afterward, 'cause once it's don... You'll be depriving Percy of his life and your three sons of a father. Be sure that's what you want. I need to hear it right now."

"Look, Percy has made my life miserable for over thirty years. I've been like a prisoner. If anyone ever deserved to die it is Percy, and if I had the guts I'd do it myself." She grabbed the Chameleon's forearm and clenched her teeth. "Spare no mercy. He has not only been a worthless husband but a worthless father as well. He won't be missed by his sons, or anyone else."

"I just needed you to be sure." He threw some bills on the table and got up. "I don't want anyone seeing us leave together. I'll go first." He strode across the bar and out onto the street.

Pastori waited with two other officers. The uniformed officers stayed by the door while Pastori walked over to where Carmen was gathering her things and preparing to leave.

"You're under arrest, Mrs. Ballard, for soliciting murder for hire."

He clamped cuffs around her wrists and escorted her out to a waiting cruiser. Before she got in, he read Carmen her Miranda rights.

She sagged momentarily with the realization of what was happening, but then seemed to square herself and appeared stoic. As she was driven away, she seemed more concerned about what was going to happen to her car than what was going to happen to her.

Later at her trial, when the Chameleon had to testify, he was astonished that she seemed so placid. She showed no remorse or anxiety about her future. He wondered if perhaps her life in jail might be preferable than what she had endured during her marriage.

This was confirmed as she was led away by the jailer. She stopped for a moment and glared at the Chameleon. "At least in prison I'll be free of that miserable son-of-a-bitch."

The CHAMELEON

"And, Percy will be safe from you," the Chameleon murmured.

CHAPTER TWENTY

The Chameleon regretted having left Meloni to fend for herself upon her arrival back in Chicago. His failure to meet her at the airport as promised had made her cold and more distant than before. Maybe her father had bent her ear. Maybe she resented the fact that he hadn't been open to her. Maybe she hated that he put his job ahead of her. Maybe all three.

The abruptness of her rejection paralyzed him and, the thought that he had squandered all that was sacred, left him in hopeless disarray. Not even prodding from his mother helped him lift his spirits from the depths of despair. All this time, he thought he was duping the world when in fact he had succeeded in only deceiving himself.

243

The CHAMELEON

His egregious disregard of the feelings of others had taken its toll. He thought of Sandy and their lives after being married, and of his daughters and all he missed in their lives. Now he had been given a second chance and he had blown it. Now it was all coming back on him as well. How could he have been so thoughtless? The conflict within him was swelling and he was second-guessing every decision he had ever made. He had been blinded by a sense of infallibility. He may have been wrong but he always thought he was right. In his maelstrom of self-righteousness, there was always a plausible explanation for his actions–an excuse. His dedication to the job was to solve one more case, to make one more bust. It was a world full of miscreants to blame, not him.

With his blurred vision, the Chameleon had failed to recognize the subtle hints which surrounded him. By filling his life with all the negative thoughts, he had left no room for the positive. He had been on a mission, but only now did he realize it was a mission of self-destruction. Undoubtedly, he had used up his nine lives and free passes. There were none left. All he could do now was hope and pray.

The Chameleon had left several messages for Meloni. She didn't return his calls. He stopped by her boutique on a windy mid-February day. "Hi," he said.

Meloni turned from the display she was arranging. "Hello," she said before turning back to her work. She was not caustic or abrasive but somewhat abrupt and impatient. She appeared preoccupied and distant. The only sign of encouragement was the engagement ring still on her finger.

Meloni avoided eye contact with the Chameleon and busied herself arranging display items.

"Looks like I've picked a busy time," the Chameleon commented.

"We're shorthanded today," Meloni replied. "Lorraine picked a bad day to be sick. It happens with her all too frequently."

"Today must be Monday," the Chameleon said. "Mondays and Fridays seem to spawn sickness."

Meloni managed her first smile. "It's reassuring to know that the Monday and Friday blues are a common curse."

When Meloni was beckoned by one of the clerks, she said, "I have to run. I'll call you after work. Will you be home this evening?"

As the Chameleon started for the door, Meloni stopped him and, in a soft voice, said, "I dreamt about you last night."

"I hope it was a good dream," the Chameleon said.

"It was!" Meloni replied and smiled. The Chameleon detected a sparkle in her eyes for the first time in a long time.

The Chameleon answered the phone on the third ring. "Hello," he said.

"Hello, Chris, I'm sorry we didn't have time to talk. Being gone so much has set me light years behind. I don't think I'll ever catch up."

"That's what happens when you're indispensable. Your employees aren't the only ones who can't get along without you. I missed you!"

"I missed you too. But you'd better get used to it. Daddy has convinced me I need to open the Lake Tahoe version of my boutique in a recently renovated wing at his hotel. That means you won't see me much in the next several months. It's an opportunity I can't pass up, and besides I don't want to disappoint my parents."

"What about me?"

"You'll survive. Besides, I think we need to cool our heels a bit. Everything has gone entirely too fast. Both of us need to catch our breaths."

The Chameleon had a flippant retort but thought the better of it. Swallowing his pride, he merely said, "I hope you are not telling me goodbye. My life would be empty without you. You know that I love you and always will."

"I love you too, Chris. If you only knew how much. Not too long ago you told me you were conflicted by some extraneous distractions and asked me to be patient and understanding. You said you would like to share them with me but couldn't at the moment. The same thing is now true for me and I'm asking you to be patient and understand. No, I'm not saying goodbye but only, 'Wait for me, I'll not be far.'"

The Chameleon could hear her sobs as the receiver clicked off. Gripped with sorrow, longing and frustration, and tormented by the thought of losing Meloni, the Chameleon could restrain himself no more. His eyes brimmed with tears that up to then had been shed only for a precious few. The performance was repeated when he met with his mother and the tearful aching would be his constant companion whenever he pined for Meloni, which proved to be most of the time.

Over the next several months, Meloni and the Chameleon spoke frequently by telephone and sporadically in person. Between some highly sensitive assignments and Meloni's frequent trips to Lake Tahoe, the Chameleon managed to weather the relationship freeze, or moratorium, as Pastori referred to it. Regardless, the hiatus was barely tolerable.

Although the two were cordial, the intimacy had faded. There was little expression of endearment. The Chameleon did not want to crowd Meloni, but at the same time his perseverance was being severely tested. All good things come to him who waits, his mother insisted. So, remembering that in the not-too-distant past Meloni had said the same thing, the Chameleon weathered the time-out in anxious anticipation.

CHAPTER TWENTY-ONE

O n March fifteenth, shortly after midnight, he received a frantic telephone call from Meloni.

"Chris! Thank God I reached you. Mom and Dad were taken hostage by Salvo Baretti. It happened at Alessandro's Italian Ristorante in my father's hotel. I was to meet them there for dinner last night, and they were waiting for me in the lobby just outside the restaurant when they were accosted by Salvo Baretti and another man by the name of Lennert Mazzenaldo."

"I know Mazzenaldo. He is a part of the Almandreo crime family in New York City. Mongo Almandreo was recently released from federal prison. I'm sorry. That's not important. Are your parents okay?"

"Just as I came into the lobby, I saw two of Daddy's security guards wrestling with the attackers. One of the security guards was shot and the other security guard shot Mazzenaldo. In the fray, Baretti was wounded but managed to grab my mother. When Daddy tried to stop them, Baretti grabbed him, too. Baretti threatened to shoot my parents if the second security guard didn't drop his weapon. Mazzenaldo was shot in the head and apparently died instantly. Baretti was bleeding badly from a shot in his upper left arm. Mom and Daddy are being held in the back room of the shop next to the restaurant. I'm not sure Mom's heart can take all of this."

"How serious is Baretti's injury?"

"He asked for a doctor. The SWAT team is negotiating for the release of my parents. Apparently, there is a standoff, as Baretti is refusing to release my parents until after he has been provided a vehicle and has safely made his get-away. We can't find a doctor willing to take the risk."

"Even if you find one, there is no guarantee that Baretti will keep his promise. The SWAT team needs to stand firm. Get the immediate release of your parents in return for medical treatment and a free pass out of Lake Tahoe."

"The authorities are reluctant to give Baretti the free pass. Their mindset seems to be to make my parents the sacrificial lambs. That way, they trade my parents' lives for Baretti's and don't risk other innocent lives."

"Everything hinges on how much Baretti values his own life. The botched kidnap attempt with two henchmen would tell me Baretti was not counting on trading his own life for a few thousand dollars."

"Chris, I want you to do the negotiating. I trust you and your judgment. I have discussed this with the authorities in Lake Tahoe and they have a plane at their disposal that will transport you. Please don't say no. If ever I needed you, it is now!"

"Of course I will come." Within the hour, the Chameleon was on his way to negotiate the release of his future in-laws. It wasn't until after they reached the Lake Tahoe Police Department that the Chameleon called Morton Weston, head of the CPD detective squad, and obtained the

CPD's approval to negotiate the release of the two kidnap victims.

Meloni met him at the LTPD. She was anxious to see him and anxious for his help. That was evident from the mixed tears of joy and profound distress he witnessed. Just seeing him and being held in his warm embrace seemed to buoy her spirits and bring her much-needed hope. The plea in her eyes was unyielding and he was willing once again to lay his life on the line, only this time not because of a sense of duty but because of a sense of unrelenting love.

Desmond Penwell, the lead negotiator for the LTPD briefed the Chameleon on the hostage situation. He had been warden of the Washington State Prison in Walla Walla for over twenty-five years and was hired on by the LTPD upon his retirement and move to Lake Tahoe. He had been credited with having rescued dozens of hostages from their criminal captors both before and after his move to Lake Tahoe. He taught hostage negotiation at various academies around the country and was a sought after speaker at various conferences including one held in Chicago which the Chameleon had attended.

The CHAMELEON

"Our negotiation attempts at obtaining the rescue of the Baranettis thus far has proven futile," Penwell told the Chameleon. "Baretti has made it clear that his demands are non-negotiable."

"What do you know about Baretti?" the Chameleon asked.

"He has a reputation of being a hardcore criminal and seems to value life, including his own, very little. Right now he is desperate."

"If he doesn't get his way, I assume he will have no hesitancy in executing his hostages."

"Correct. If he is expendable, so are they."

"That narrows down the options, doesn't it?"

"Absolutely. I don't think any of us are willing to trade the lives of two innocent hostages for the life of an insidious villain."

"Especially these two hostages," the Chameleon said.

"Especially these two," Penwell acknowledged and winked.

When the plain clothes detectives admitted Dr. Roberto Lampiere into the now deserted lobby in front of Galley Creations at Carleono's Holiday Casino & Resort, he was no longer a bespectacled diminutive figure of a man but a six foot-five inch, two hundred and twenty-five pound "medical doctor." With a white lab coat and stethoscope dangling from around his neck, and a name tag, the Chameleon was admitted into Galley Creations by a wave of a .40 Glock semi-automatic that Baretti had trained in the Chameleon's direction.

Baretti was holding his damaged arm and wincing. He was attempting to adjust an improvised tourniquet consisting of a handkerchief and ball point pen. The whole left side of his body was soaked in blood. He did not seem to be faring well. Baretti was a muscled bear of a man with a ruddy complexion scared by acne. His face was dominated by a prominent nose developed through heavy alcohol consumption through the years and dark, piercing eyes full of hatred, contempt and ridicule. It was obvious to the Chameleon that he was dealing with a genuine desperado.

Since Baretti's arm was bleeding on both sides it was obvious the bullet had exited the arm. The way Baretti's left arm was dangling, the Chameleon surmised that the slug had hit the humerus. That was borne out by the Chameleon's subsequent examination. The amount of blood on Baretti's clothing indicated that the path of the slug travelled through some critical vessels. There was no way for Baretti to mask the pain and torment.

"Empty the contents of your medical bag onto the counter so that I can see what you have," Baretti ordered.

The Chameleon carefully removed two syringes containing clear fluids and placed them gently on the counter.

"What are those for?" Baretti asked.

"One is a local anesthetic. The other is a pain killer." In reality, both contained a general anesthetic that would induce the loss of consciousness.

When the Chameleon mentioned pain killer, Baretti nodded. "What are you waiting for?"

"These should do the trick," the Chameleon said as he removed the caps from the needles.

As the Chameleon started to inject Baretti with the contents of the two syringes, Baretti said, "These won't knock me out cause if they do, you will die with the hostages."

Without hesitating, the Chameleon injected him with the contents of the two syringes. Almost immediately Baretti dropped the weapon and sank to the floor.

When the Chameleon, first entered Galley Creations, Carleono was bound to a chair by several silk scarves that had been part of the shop's inventory. Apparently, Baretti felt Magdalena posed no threat, as she sat on a chair next to her husband without restraints.

Although the Chameleon did not look in their direction, he could see the two out of the corner of his eye. Their look upon recognizing their liberator was priceless. He could see they were startled but quick to stifle their true reactions.

He untied Carleono and, with Magdalena in his arms ushered the two to safety. The SWAT team secured the scene and summoned the paramedics who, accompanied by police personnel, transported their sleeping beauty to the ER at St. Lucy's Hospital.

Carleono and Magdalena, along with the Chameleon, were taken to the penthouse suite atop Carleono's Holiday Casino & Resort. There they were joined by Cyrus Townsend, the LTPD Chief of Police, who personally presented a dazed, distraught and a soon to be relieved Meloni. Chief Townsend left the room so that the four could savor the moment.

Meloni, immediately upon being admitted, rushed to her parents who were huddled together at the far end of the main room. "Are you two all right?" she asked anxiously. The two nodded and the three embraced.

When the Chameleon cleared his throat, Meloni turned her head and, as their eyes met, rushed into his waiting arms. "Thank you," she sobbed as she held him tight.

Returning to her parents, Meloni just shook her head and said, "I can't believe you made it. I've been sick with worry."

"We owe Chris our lives," Magdalena said managing a smile.

"He is a brave man," Carleono added as he beckoned for the Chameleon to come closer.

"We've got to quit meeting like this," the Chameleon said as the four hung onto each other and uttered a thankful prayer.

Meanwhile, a groggy Baretti was trying to recover from the double dose of lullaby juice. In his stupor he became quite talkative and disclosed he was carrying out a hit order on Carleono that had been issued by his boss, Mongo Almandreo. The motive: to prevent Carleono from revealing incriminating evidence to his future son-in-law who was a CPD detective concerning his boss' involvement in the assassination of the meddlesome FBI agent in New York City in 1965.

Out of harm's way and now in the serenity of the Baranetti mansion, Carleono and Magdalena had a new-found affection for the Chameleon. They viewed him in a different light. He had risked his life for them and they owed their lives to him. Carleono knew that meant that it was now time to lay all the cards on the table and let the chips fall where they may. They owed that much at least to the man who had just saved their lives.

Carleono's told the Chameleon his life history. He left nothing out and included all the sordid details he had provided to his wife and daughter. Carleono looked at the Chameleon with tears in his eyes. "Chris, we owe you an apology."

"No apologies necessary," the Chameleon responded.

"No. I prejudged you without giving you an opportunity to explain yourself."

The Chameleon shrugged and smiling at Carleono said, "I am guilty of the same thing."

"Ordinarily, I am not one to jump to conclusions. Everyone has a right to be heard and present their side. I denied you that opportunity and for that I am truly sorry."

"I, as well," Magdalena said.

Before the Chameleon could respond, Carleono said, "My treasures are not the wealth I have acquired. In fact, as we speak, I have my attorney and accountant trying to find ways to make it help others who perhaps need a miracle in their lives. My wife and daughter are my treasures.

They are all that matter." With that, Carleono turned his face away and reached for his handkerchief. When the Chameleon tried to console him, he murmured, "I'll be okay. I just want Meloni to be happy."

The Chameleon put his arms around the man he hoped someday would be his father-in-law. With Carleono's vulnerability having been exposed, the Chameleon experienced a closeness he had not felt since the death of his father.

"You represent the son I never had," Carleono managed to say after several agonizing minutes. "Magdalena and I entrusted you with our lives and now, we entrust you with the life of our only child, our daughter, Meloni." Placing his hand on the Chameleon's shoulder, he added, "You have our blessing to marry our daughter." Meloni and the Chameleon squeezed each other's hand and kissed.

"We learned from Chief Townsend," Carleono said, "that our abductor was employed by Mongo Almendreo to eliminate me, apparently out of fear that I would blow the whistle on his criminal escapades and involvement in the death of your father. I am willing to do that now if given the opportunity. His botched attempt in assassinating me and presumably my wife as well nullifies what has up to now been considered a sacred and ironclad pledge of silence on my part. In other words, all bets are now off, at least as far as the Almendreo faction is concerned."

"The chief," the Chameleon responded, "also stated that the motive for the hit, according to Baretti, was the supposition that you would be revealing incriminating evidence to me. The only person to whom I ever revealed our connection was a retired FBI agent who was my father's partner at the time of his death."

"Lex Stedman?"

The Chameleon was stunned. "How did you know that?" he asked.

"I knew Lex when he was on the take back in 1964 and 1965. He provided me and the heads of other crime families, including Almandreo, with some highly sensitive information. He, more than anyone else kept all the gaming people alerted to potential raids. What Lex made on the side was probably twice his salary as an FBI agent."

The Chameleon just looked down sadly and pensively and shook his head. Lex Stedman had been a person the Chameleon's mother had confided in and depended on. In fact, the family's whole future literally was held in the palms of Lex Stedman's hands. The effect the revelation would have on his mother was something that the Chameleon didn't want to think about, especially not now. In his mind, Lex came from the same mold as Judas, Brutus and Benedict Arnold. Lex had clearly sold his soul to the devil and for that a price would have to be exacted.

"Are you all right?" Meloni whispered.

"Not really," he said. "Lex was someone we all had learned to trust and rely on. He was a father figure. It would almost be as devastating as finding out there was no God."

Carleono asked, "Am I correct in assuming that it was fairly recently that you disclosed what Lex obviously considered to be an unholy alliance?"

"Yes," the Chameleon responded. "I had kept my relationship with Meloni and thus with you a secret up to several weeks ago. I thought it was important to be candid with him, since I trusted him and had set my sights on you as the prime figure behind my father's death."

263

The CHAMELEON

"All the pieces are coming together except for one," Carleono said, "and I will tell you what that is in a minute. Lex Stedman has kept his finger in the pie and has remained in the inner circle despite his retirement from the FBI. He is still a valuable asset to Mongo Almandreo and still on his payroll, I would assume. Revealing to Almandreo our perceived threatening alliance would be proof of his allegiance to Almandreo, thus guaranteeing what he would consider job security. Knowing that Baretti was a hit man for Almandreo provides the last piece in the puzzle."

"What is the missing piece you referred to?" the Chameleon asked.

"How you targeted me as the person behind your father's death warrant."

Before the Chameleon could reply, Carleono added, "There is something more pressing that we all need to know, especially your fiancée. Was your setting your sights on me, as you framed it, something that preceded your relationship with Meloni, or did you establish the relationship as a means to infiltrate her family and thus gather evidence against me?"

"If you're asking if my meeting Meloni was a pretext to gather information about her father, the answer is an unequivocal and categorical no. You weren't even a blip on my radar screen. I didn't even know her maiden name when we first met. I fell in love head over heels with a woman at first sight, a woman who I didn't know and a woman who immediately pervaded my whole being. When I rescued you and Magdalena, I still thought you were behind my father's execution. I put my life on the line mainly out of the deep love I have for Meloni. And, I'd do it all over again, even if I had not been convinced that my rush to judgment as to your involvement in my father's death was flawed."

By the manner in which she peered into his eyes and clasped his hands, the Chameleon knew Meloni believed him. From that moment, neither doubted the other's love or motives. Nor, did Meloni's parents ever again entertain any thoughts to the contrary.

The Chameleon continued. "I was at the Iceman's bedside after Lex called me. The Iceman wanted to clear his conscience in his final hours and speak to a relative of the slain FBI agent. He admitted to having killed my father and fingered the DOJ as the source of his commission. I was unfamiliar with the DOJ and was told by Lex that DOJ was an acronym for Dispenser of Justice. He said the concept for what he called the tribunal was the brainchild of a law school dropout. When you and I first met, you talked about having dropped out of law school. I didn't think too much of it then until I discovered that in 1965 the Iceman had been employed by your bar and grill. That, together with what I considered some other telltale signs relayed to me by Lex, led me in your direction. My mother tried to tell me I had a defective compass but I was blinded by my compulsion to solve my father's murder. In my mindlessness, I failed to look outside the square. Like the attorney who representing himself is deemed to have a fool for a client, I failed to see the forest because of the trees. Forgive me for my complete lack of objectivity and for having placed my faith in the wrong person. I give you my word it won't happen again."

"There's another question that needs to be answered," Magdalena said, breaking her long silence, "When's the wedding?"

"Not soon enough." Meloni responded as her and the Chameleon's lips met, marking the prelude to an epic starlit night that would carry them into a whole new dimension and beyond.

CHAPTER TWENTY-TWO

The unholy alliance, as Carleono termed it, was no doubt perceived by Lex Stedman as a threat to all the shadowy exploits he had kept hidden virtually his whole career as an FBI agent. Exposing his sellout of a fellow FBI agent was bad enough, but to have sealed the fate of his friend and partner and have it broadcast to the whole world was abhorrent and inexcusable.

It was more out of a sense of protecting his own image than proving his loyalty to Mongo Almandreo that Lex Stedman alerted his benefactor to the possibility that the Chameleon, by marrying into the Baranetti family, would pose a threat to the sanctity of Mafia. Lex Stedman, by being Almandreo's good and faithful servant, his 'ears' and adviser, was persuasive in convincing Almandreo that Carleono could no longer be trusted. He insisted Carleono would sooner rather than later reveal to his son-in-law the secrets of the past. The risk that they would all be exposed as conspirators in the unsolved execution of an FBI agent in 1965 was more than problematic, considering that the son of the slain FBI agent was not only marrying the daughter of the man who knew the answer to the riddle of who killed his father, but who himself was an undercover police officer. The mix was a recipe for disaster, and Carleono needed to be silenced before it was too late.

Lex Stedman knew that there was no statute of limitations on a first-degree murder charge. He also had followed closely the botched kidnap attempt of Carleono and his wife and was made privy to the statements of Salvo Baretti implicating Almandreo. He knew it would not be long before Carleono would return the favor. Since he no longer had any allegiance to Almandreo, it was just a matter of time before Carleono let the cat out of the bag. Since the cat included Lex, Lex's complicity was now in peril. Everything suddenly was blowing up in his face.

The CHAMELEON

Lex knew all too well what the consequences would be if he was exposed. Being subjected to public disgrace and ridicule, castigation or worse by Almandreo and having to face the widow and family of his slain partner, Lex began considering the alternatives. He was leaning towards what he considered to be the only viable alternative.

Lex had been flirting with disaster ever since he became a double agent. He was an insider as far as the FBI was concerned, and he was an insider as far as Almandreo was concerned. Neither side had questioned his loyalty. Both entrusted him with classified and top secret information. He was not at all bashful about sharing that information if it suited his needs.

Bruno Trosconi and Foss Evans, the Nevada-based FBI agents assigned to the abduction of Carleono and Magdalena, were unwitting informants, and provided Lex with a blow-by-blow account of the bungled attempt on Carleono's life. They had also informed Lex that for some inexplicable reason Almandreo had decided to take a powder. The authorities were stymied in trying to execute the federal warrant for

Almandreo's arrest. Whoever alerted Almandreo was a matter of speculation.

It was Memorial Day weekend when Della called her husband to the telephone. On the other end was Bruno Trosconi.

"Lex," Trosconi said, "I hate to interrupt your solitude. However, the special agent in charge, Chad Stoner, would like to visit with you and has asked that I set up an appointment for the two of you to meet. Apparently, it has to do with the Baranetti abduction."

"I don't know how I can help," Lex said. "Everything I know is unofficial and hearsay. You know more than I do."

Lex's hands were now becoming clammy and he began to feel the all too familiar churning in the pit of his stomach. "When does he want to meet?" Lex managed to ask.

"As soon as you can come down here," Trosconi responded.

"It won't be until tomorrow since it's late in the day and I'm in the middle of a project."

"Unless you hear otherwise, we will look forward to seeing you at headquarters at ten a.m. tomorrow."

"See you then," Lex said.

After he hung up the telephone, he wiped his damp palms on his pant leg and gazed into the quizzical eyes of Della, his wife of over fifty years. "Stoner wants to pick my brain on God knows what," Lex said looking away.

"That's what happens when you're indispensable," Della said reaching for his hand and squeezing it. "You're shaking," she said. "Don't tell me they need you to come in today. That's pretty inconsiderate."

Unable to find the right words, Lex went to the master bedroom where he shaved, showered and changed clothes. Imprinted in his mind was Della's cherub face that radiated her unremitting love, innocence and unsuspecting loyalty.

Lex led Della to believe he was headed to the bureau office. He bid her a goodbye and told her the intrusion on their day would be temporary. Unbeknownst to her, the two looked into each other's eyes and held each other for the last time.

The sun hung low in the sky as he headed in the direction of the Catskill Mountains. Lex drove with purpose, knowing that all his misdeeds had finally caught up with him. The gig was up.

There was nowhere to turn and he was *not* going to spend the rest of his life in prison. He grimaced as his mind conjured the image of becoming the sexual object of a gang of prison thugs.

The stars studded a cloudless canopy of sky and only the moon bore witness to the lone vehicle that sat perched on a precipice, its engine idling. Lex sat for a moment in mute resignation, then rolled the nose of the car to the very edge. He held it there with his foot on the brake as his eyes swept the darkness. Moments later the passenger compartment was illuminated by an orange flash and the muffled report of a single shot. At the same moment the vehicle lurched forward and plunged into the ravine exploding into a ball of flames when it hit the rocky bottom. It would be more than a month before the wreckage was discovered. The Chameleon, for one, felt it would have better if Lex had never been born.

CHAPTER TWENTY-THREE

C arleono considered the attempt on his and his wife's life a declaration of war by Almandreo. No longer did he feel compelled to honor the unwritten code of silence and loyalty as it applied to Mongo Almandreo. Almandreo clearly was acting on his own and his actions in no way could or would be imputed to the other crime families. In other words, Carleono knew nothing about the Rigoletti family or its successor or the Fredanado family or its predecessor. If he did, he now had a sudden lapse of memory.

Almandreo seemed to have dropped off the face of the earth. Although there were sightings as far away as Caracas, they could not be substantiated. Wherever he might have gone, he left no tracks.

Salvo Baretti, confronted with his prior statements, continued to sing like a canary and was jailed to ensure his safety and availability. In exchange for his cooperation and guilty pleas to two counts of attempted kidnapping, he was sentenced to two twenty-year consecutive sentences to be served at a location to be determined by the federal government. In the interim, the recuperating Baretti would await the capture and prosecution of Almandreo and enjoy the hospitality of the federal government.

With Baretti's help, it was easy for the authorities to trace all calls to and from Baretti's cell phone in Nevada to and from Almandreo's cell phone in New York. The cell tower pings verified the calls and pinpointed the exact location of the callers throughout the entire siege.

Baretti told authorities, "I was only following orders. Almandreo orchestrated the whole negotiation process."

Lennox Sinclair, an agent with the Nevada Bureau of Investigation, was recording Baretti's statement. "Are you saying the give-no-quarter strategy was Almandreo's and you were just acting as his puppet?"

"I worked for Almandreo and only did what I was ordered to do. Nothing more and nothing less."

"Would you have executed your hostages if Almandreo had ordered it?"

"It would have been them or me!"

It was through this interstate connection that the FBI became involved. Almandreo was an accessory both before and during the fact. Almandreo aided and abetted the perpetration of the offense of kidnap, false imprisonment, assault and attempted murder. And, under the felony murder rule, the death of Baretti's confederate, Lennert Mazzenaldo, could be imputed to both Baretti and Almandreo. Because the conspiracy and perpetration crossed state lines, the feds acquired jurisdiction even though both federal and state personnel were involved. Out of courtesy and deference, however, the two entities acted in concert and respected each other's authority.

So as not to implicate himself, Carleono had his Nevada attorney, Zeblin Wrenada, negotiate with both the feds and the state in his behalf. By providing information about Almandreo, Carleono did not want to implicate himself. Thanks to Wrenada's efforts, Carleono was granted transactional immunity from both governmental entities. That meant that neither what Carleono said or anything connected with the subject of what was said could in any way be used against him and he was immune from prosecution on any and all matters connected to the case.

Carleono spent the better part of two weeks meeting with the federal and state authorities. He was able to provide some critical information that would form the kaleidoscopic pattern of guilt for his old nemesis, Mongo Almandreo. He was able to do this without having to burn his two childhood buddies, Evon Rigoletti and Ezio Fredanado. Wrenada's skillful negotiation also prevented the authorities from asking any questions about the so-called Mafia tribunal.

The Chameleon was also called back to Lake Tahoe to meet with both the federal and state authorities, including the U.S. attorney and the state prosecuting attorney. This provided the perfect opportunity for Meloni to accompany the Chameleon. While Carleono and the Chameleon attended to the business at hand, Meloni and her mother busied themselves with what would be billed as the wedding of the century. Even the Lake Tahoe branch of Meloni's boutique was put on hold so as not to divert their attention.

Even though Mongo Almandreo seemingly had vanished into thin air, the authorities were able to erase his crime family from the map, thanks to the leads provided by Carleono and Salvo Baretti. It was Baretti's testimony that provided the nail for the notorious crime family's coffin. Unfortunately, his testimony exacted a heavy price. Barely into two years of incarceration, Baretti had an unfortunate accident in the exercise pen while bench pressing two-hundred-pound weights. For some inexplicable reason, while returning the weight bar to its resting place above his head, the pins to both side posts popped, collapsing the columns, causing the bar and weights to crush Baretti's neck.

Having received full immunity for his cooperation, Carleono didn't have to keep looking over his shoulder and was heralded as a hero of sorts. Almandreo's competition divided the territorial spoils, and were grateful to Carleono for his having upheld the code of silence and loyalty as to them.

278

The Chameleon was most modest about his involvement in the liberation of his future in-laws and causing Almandreo's house of cards to tumble. He had received nation-wide attention for his heroism and protested his awards and recognition by proclaiming he was only doing his job. In the process, he earned the respect of all those who mattered most and then some.

Meloni and the Chameleon's mother would continue to be his staunchest supporters and fans. So would his daughters. *All's well that ends well,* he thought.

With his father's death solved and the exoneration of Carleono, the Chameleon felt liberated in a way he never thought possible. He had a new lease on life. Though he had been someone who had helped turn some of the societal windmills right side up, now he could enjoy the fruits of his toil and the good things God had in store for him. Without some pending case or role to assume, he could now turn his full attention to a more pleasant preoccupation–Meloni.

CHAPTER TWENTY-FOUR

2008

Right after their engagement, Meloni and the Chameleon began discussing the annulment process in the Catholic Church with respect to their prior marriages. It was important to both that they be married in the church and that their marriage be recognized by the church as valid. Neither was sure sufficient grounds existed to obtain annulments in their respective situations.

"Don't be such a skeptic," Meloni said as the two traveled north on Lake Shore Drive. "If it worked for Daddy, it can work for us."

"Your father's situation was different," the Chameleon said. "I was married for fifteen years and had two children. If I wasn't married in the eyes of the church, then my daughters were born out of wedlock and you know what that means."

"My first marriage was also in the church."

"Yes, but you had no children."

"Shouldn't make any difference."

"How is either one of us going to be able to argue lack of intent to marry, fraud, duress, undue influence or any of the other recognizable grounds needed to obtain an annulment?"

"How about insanity? When I married Devon, I was told by my parents and all my friends that I was crazy."

"Sounds like you're about to make the same mistake."

"Well, I am insanely in love with you."

"And, I with you. You know I am crazy in love with you."

"That would make for a great song," Meloni said as she pulled into the parking lot at the rectory of Our Lady of Mount Carmel Catholic Church.

On the third ring, the door was opened by the housekeeper and the two were ushered into Father Jonathon O'Shaunessy's study. As they wcrc announced, Father O'Shaunessy rose and shook their hands.

"The Carcellis have been parishioners and close friends of mine for a number of years," Father O'Shaunessy said. "In fact, I baptized both of Chris' daughters."

"What kind of chance do we have?" the Chameleon asked.

"Can't even give you an indication until I've met with each of you. And, even then, it's difficult to predict."

The Chameleon just shook his head.

"I take you are not optimistic," Father O'Shaunessy said.

"I can't in good conscience say that I entered into my marriage with Sandy blindly or that I was forced to do so."

Father O'Shaunessy then handed each of them a booklet entitled Annulments and the Catholic Church.

The Chameleon looked only briefly at the booklet and set it aside. "I can't believe divorce dooms one to hell or that the Judge of the Universe is persuaded by technicalities."

"Chris," Father O'Shaunessy replied, "you work with the law every day. If there were no rules, there would be utter chaos. If those rules weren't enforced, they would be worthless. The same is true of the canon law. They have a purpose and are to be observed. If you are asking if divorced people, who remarry, go to hell, I would have to say no. Our God is a loving and merciful God. However, we have to obey his commands as best we can and that is why I have offered to help you and Meloni obtain annulments."

"My only point," the Chameleon persisted, "is that where the parties enter into marriage with their eyes wide open and are not forced to do so and where both understand the natural and probable consequences of their actions, how can the church say there was no valid marriage?"

"You make a good point," Father O'Shaunessy said, "especially where you and Sandy consummated the marriage, producing two offspring, and lived together as husband and wife for over fifteen years. All I can say is pray and trust in the Lord."

"I have prayed," the Chameleon responded. "And, I do trust in the Lord. To be honest, I'm not hopeful."

"Annulments have been granted in some improbable cases. Without knowing the particulars, I can't say for certain. After you have filled out these forms and I have spoken with each of you, I will have a better idea. Remember, posturing is transparent to the One who created you. He is incapable of being fooled."

After the two filled out the forms and spoke in private with Father O'Shaunessy, the Chameleon left feeling uncertain as to whether his prior marriage would be declared a nullity. Meloni was more optimistic and tried to encourage the Chameleon. "It is now in God's hands."

Something that was not debatable was where the wedding would be held. For a number of reasons, St. Patrick's Cathedral in New York City was the church of choice. Operating under the assumption that the annulments would be granted or other dispensations given, St. Patrick's

Cathedral was booked for Saturday, June twentieth, two thousand nine at two p.m. That was a long way off and would allow the annulment process to run its course and allow for ample planning in either event.

"Why are you staring at me like that, Superman?" Meloni asked as the two sat across from each other while Adriana cleared the dishes from the breakfast nook in her small apartment.

"I was wondering what would happen if one or both of us were denied an annulment," he replied.

"If you're asking if I would still marry you, the answer is still yes. How many times are you going to ask me that?"

"I was just wondering," the Chameleon replied as Adriana came back into the room with fresh brew.

"Wondering what?" Adriana asked as she filled the Chameleon's coffee cup.

"Nothing really," he responded.

"He's still doubting whether our annulments will be granted and asking me that same old question," Meloni said as she held her cup out for a refill.

"For heaven's sake, Chris," Adriana blurted, "if worse comes to worse we can have a ceremony performed where the reception is held."

"But I thought . . ."

Before the Chameleon could complete his statement, Adriana interrupted. "Never mind what I think. God is not going to frown if your wedding is not a Catholic wedding or is not held at St. Patrick's Cathedral. Obviously, that is what we are all hoping for and is probably what is going to happen. If it doesn't, I don't think that should change your plans to marry."

"I can't believe I'm hearing you say that," the Chameleon said as he stood and placed his arms around his mother.

"Not so rough. You're going to spill the coffee on my freshly waxed floor."

"Sorry. But you're the one who insisted on a Catholic wedding."

"If it's all right with Meloni, it's all right with me."

"It is," Meloni said. "It's meant to be."

"Have you started preparing your guest list yet," Adriana asked.

Meloni looked at Chris and then at Adriana. "Chris and I have talked about that. We've concluded there are many who would be offended if they weren't invited. We've estimated there will be anywhere from four to five hundred by the time the list is complete."

"Just counting the relatives from the two sides of the family, there will be over one hundred," the Chameleon added.

"My goodness!" Adriana exclaimed. "If the list gets any bigger, we'll have to book Soldier Field."

"Don't laugh, it might happen!" the Chameleon said looking at Meloni.

"Don't give me that look! It's your old cronies who will come just for the drinks."

"I stand corrected," the Chameleon said. "But who is it that wants a formal wedding?"

"Not you or daddy but everyone else."

"Including me," Adriana said raising her hand in the air.

The CHAMELEON

"It appears I'm outnumbered," the Chameleon said. "I suppose it will be a white tie affair."

"Only to aggravate you, darling," Meloni said as she planted a kiss on the Chameleon's forehead.

"Do you still plan to hire professionals to assist in the planning phase?" the Chameleon asked.

"Yes. I don't think you or I or our mothers have the time or expertise."

"If the wedding is at St. Patrick's Cathedral, Meloni's father has agreed to transport the guests from New York to Lake Tahoe and back by private jet," the Chameleon told his mother.

"Not *if*, Superman, but *when*," Meloni corrected. "Remember, if God is with us no one can be against us!"

The Miras had changed their names and relocated to prevent what happened to Donato Leonardo Mira to happen to them. Originally, it was thought that the whole family was a target. Changing their names and being uprooted was no easy matter then and certainly not now. After all these years, they were faced with still another dilemma, whether to change their names back.

It was common knowledge, in the law enforcement community at least, that the Chameleon, the hero in the liberation of the Baranettis, was the son of Donato Leonardo Mira, the FBI agent killed by the Almandreo crime family in New York City in 1965. It was just a matter of time before it would be exposed in the media that Christopher Claudio Carcelli was in reality Donato Leonardo Mira Jr., a decorated undercover detective employed by the Chicago Police Department.

The Chameleon's days as an undercover officer seemed numbered. Notoriety was an undercover officer's kiss-of-death and the Chameleon's success no doubt would be his undoing. He had done his job too well. Just how long he could continue to be effective in his current capacity, only time would tell.

Before the Carcellis had time to deliberate on the effect of the recent events, the media had a heyday with their exposure of the real identities of the Carcellis. Receiving notoriety state-wide and maybe even nationally was predictable, but internationally? The Carcellis thought it was not newsworthy, at least not so as to receive worldwide attention. They were wrong and were suddenly thrust into the global limelight. Both the print and electronic media at home and abroad made pests of themselves. The Chameleon's covert activities abruptly came to an end. And, much to their chagrin, all the Carcellis became instant celebrities.

Although who they were was no longer a best-kept secret, the Carcellis were reluctant to undergo a name change. The Carcellis now collectively considered a hyphenated version in light of the exposure, either Carcelli-Mira or Mira-Carcelli. Because their legal name for over forty years had been Carcelli, and the considerable red tape to change their names on everything from driver's licenses to Social Security numbers to bank accounts to credit cards to professional licenses to diplomas to birth certificates, they opted to stick with their current name. Whether their alias was Mira or Carcelli, they were uncertain. What the three sons did know, however, was that they would always cherish their ancestral names, including their rightful birth names.

The Chameleon had had a plethora of pen names during his years as an undercover officer with the CPD. However, he never considered the name on his badge to be a pen name. As Christopher Claudio Carcelli, he had earned the respect of his peers and everyone else in the criminal justice system and it was a name to revere. As a descendant of Donato Leonardo Mira, he was proud of his lineage. His father's St. Christopher medal validated his assumed first name and he had never felt he had desecrated or diluted the family tree. What he was was much more important than what he was called.

The CHAMELEON

    With his cover blown, the Chameleon could no longer operate incognito. He felt like an outcast but was soon integrated into the administrative branch of the CPD detective squad. Normally, at least in the business world, the rule was that you don't take your best salesman off the floor and put him or her in the back office. Here, the CPD had no choice.

    The Chameleon didn't have time to get bored. In May of 2008, the chief of police of the Chicago Police Department retired. Morton Weston was appointed acting chief and ultimately the permanent chief. That left a vacancy to head up the crack detective squad. The CPD didn't need to look very far, however, for Weston's replacement. The Chameleon was appointed as head of the CPD detective squad. Not bad for a guy who had just turned fifty. He was not ready for the dry dock.

CHAPTER TWENTY-FIVE

2009

Just across the street from the main entrance to St. Patrick's Cathedral, the place Meloni and the Chameleon had chosen to be married, is a metal sculpture of the world resting on the shoulders of a Titan known only as Atlas. His great burden is patently obvious by the artist's rendition. The subliminal effect on the viewer is inexplicable. No one walks away without absorbing some of Atlas's strain and pain. How long the burden lingers is subjective and speculative. It is all thought to be in the mind of the beholder.

What was predictable, however, was the weight that lifted from the Chameleon's shoulders upon receiving a telephone call on Wednesday, less than two days short of a year marking the anniversary of his engagement to Meloni.

"Chris, this is Father Jonathon. I have just received word from the Judicial Vicar that your petition for annulment has been granted. On the basis of the sworn statements submitted by Sandy, yourself and the other affiants, it was determined that in the eyes of the church the two of you had entered into an invalid marriage. Beyond that, I have been provided no other explanation or basis for the decree. Apparently, that will be included in the official document you will be receiving in the mail."

"What about Meloni?"

"Because that is privileged, I can only divulge that information to her. As soon as I hang up, I will be telephoning her."

"By that, I assume a decision has been made in reference to her petition."

"Right you are. Hopefully, you are pleased with the determination in reference to your case. I know it is important to you, Meloni, and each of your parents."

"Father, I can't thank you enough. Just when I think life can't get better, it does. Why the Lord has been favoring me, I don't know, but I just hope it continues. God knows, however, that I don't deserve it."

"Our Creator didn't breathe life into us to feed us to the wolves. He is with us always, even when we reject him and trudge into the forbidden. It is not He who has created the schism and the separation, but us. And, it is we who must reach out for his outstretched hands and grasp them. He is yearning for our embrace. When we submit, life becomes easier."

"I guess some of us have learned that the hard way. Although it has taken me literally a half century to realize it, we have to forgive to be forgiven. Maybe, I have opened a door to be forgiven by forgiving those connected with my father's death."

"By doing that, you have made room for all the good things God has in store for you. Up to recently, you apparently had blocked the passage to the Lord. With that impediment removed and the impediment to your marriage no longer a concern, your destiny is pretty much in your hands, or should I say in God's hands, if you follow his spiritual compass."

"I intend to do just that. Not only have I made a mess of my life by doing it mainly my way, but by putting it in God's hands I have made life, as you say, so much easier and more predictable. It is comforting to know that someone up there is looking out for me."

"That way you don't need to keep looking over your shoulder."

"If only you knew! If only you knew!"

It seemed like an eternity before the Chameleon received the telephone call from Meloni. In reality, it was but minutes.

"Hello, Superman," Meloni said in her usual saucy voice. "I just received a call from Father Jonathon. He said he had just spoken with you. However, he refused to disclose the church's decision with reference to your petition." Then silence.

"Do you realize that suspense is detrimental to my health? Are you trying to give me a heart attack?"

"Whatever do you mean, dear?"

"I mean if I don't take a breath in the next second or two, my cause of death with be listed as asphyxia. Or, should I not die from asphyxia, I will most certainly be afflicted wholly and permanently by the calamity the mind sorcerers refer to fondly as acute anxiety."

"The tone in Father Jonathon's voice tells me you made the cut. And, in case you are interested, he has confirmed that I have likewise. So, why all the anguish?"

"Just paranoia on my part, I guess."

"Oh, ye of little faith."

With emotions jettisoned and another hurdle cleared, Meloni and the Chameleon were gliding into an ever-fascinating life together. The good news would soon be shared with Meloni's parents and the Chameleon's mother. Life was not good; it was great!

CHAPTER TWENTY-SIX

T he white marble and majestic Gothic spires of St. Patrick's Cathedral gleamed in the sunlight of a picture perfect New York morning. The church resembled a precious antique gem set amidst the glittering glass high-rise structures that looked down on it. Across the street by Rockefeller Center, hotdog and coffee vendors were just setting up for the day. Meanwhile, the wedding planner and his staff of nearly forty workers had been bustling around since 5:00 a.m. unloading flower arrangements, bouquets, ribbon and reams of tulle and satin draping.

It wasn't just the splendor of the famous New York landmark. It was a place that had special meaning. It was here that the three sons of Donato Leonardo Mira were christened. Coincidentally, it was also where the only daughter of Dante Carleono Baranetti was christened two

298

months after Meloni's birth. Now it would be the place where two lives would join together as one when Meloni and the Chameleon would become man and wife.

By that afternoon, St. Patrick's Cathedral was decked in mounds of blossoms lining the center aisle of the church. Graceful satin and tulle bows hung from each pew. At the front of the sanctuary were two tapered candelabras and a semi-circle of beautifully arranged flowers nesting in a graceful bed of ferns along the full length of the altar. The smell of flowers greeted the guests even before they walked into the building. Ushers in black tailored suits escorted people to their seats. An impressive string orchestra and vocalist serenaded the waiting throng while behind the scene, the wedding party scurried around getting dressed and ready for the ceremony.

In his first wedding, the Chameleon had bypassed both of his brothers as best men. Whether out of a desire not to have to choose between the two or in an attempt to reward his friend and fellow detective, Rolland Harken, for having introduced him to Sandy, neither Franc nor Tony was invited to be best man. He always regretted that decision. This time, things would be different. Both would be his "best men." No misperceptions here. Partly in an attempt to somewhat balance the attendance on the groom's side, and mostly to find a prominent place in the wedding party for Sal's two sons, Rocco and Ricco were added as groomsmen, as were the Chameleon's nephews, Randy and Blake.

The men in the wedding party were smartly decked out in white dinner jackets over black trousers. The white pleated shirts with turn-down collars, gold studs and cufflinks were accented by matching cummerbunds and bow ties. Gleaming black patent leather shoes finished off the ensemble.

Meloni chose Lenna to be her matron of honor, and Caitlin, Chelsea and Lisha, together with three of her friends since childhood, to be her bridesmaids. Lenna and the bridesmaids wore full-length strapless gowns. The rich black satin softly flared from waist to hem. Floor-length sashes of white satin cascaded from large bows at the back of the waist. Each wore velvet pumps with white bows.

As Meloni was getting ready, her mother had come into the dressing room clutching two purple satin bags. Retrieving the contents, she had said to Meloni, "These belonged to your great grandmother. My mother wore them at her wedding, as did I. Now it's your turn."

Meloni fingered the necklace and wondered who would be next in the long line of succession.

Suddenly a hush fell over the crowd as the musicians stopped playing, and two altar boys ceremoniously made their way down the aisle and lit the candelabras situated on either side of the chancel. Prior to the processional, the mothers of the bride and groom each lit a small candle on each side of the Unity candle that the bride and groom would light at the end of the ceremony.

Meanwhile, the wedding party gathered at the back of the church nervously waiting for the music to start again. As the violins sent out their sweet strains, two-by-two the wedding party made its way to the front the sanctuary. As they reached the front, the ladies moved to the left and the men to the right. The Chameleon stood waiting for his bride. He could feel his heart pounding in his chest and dampness on his palms.

Suddenly, the Kilgren and Chancel organs began to play together, filling the sanctuary with sound of the *Wedding March*. The music rolled and reverberated magnificently from the vaulted ceiling. The entire assembly rose to its feet. Smiling faces peered expectantly toward the vestibule.

Meloni clasped her father's arm and gazed down the full length of the rose-colored carpet that waited to receive her. She clung to him as he gently kissed her on the forehead. "Are you as nervous as I am?" he asked.

"You have no idea," she replied. "Just don't let go of me."

Her eyes captured the face of the man who waited for her at the front of the church. She saw his face—the way he looked at her—and tears welled in her eyes. Her father squeezed her arm. She felt her feet and her father's strength carry her forward as she made her way down the aisle. Light streamed through the Great Rose transom behind her and surrounded her in a pool of light. Bathed in streams of radiance, Meloni stood out like the sun on a clear summer day.

Her hair was twisted into a soft chignon. A graceful veil cascaded from a diamond-studded tiara. It flowed over her white satin gown and elegant train. The form-fitting strapless bodice and dress was intricately studded with seed pearls and hand-sewn sequins. She carried a bouquet of velvety white Gardenias, and looked like an angel.

Upon reaching the chancel steps, the processional music stopped. Wearing his colorful ceremonial vestments, The Most Reverend Donovan McKenzie, the Archbishop of New York would perform the ceremony. To Meloni, the Chameleon, looked every bit the handsome prince, as he descended the steps to meet his bride and her father. The Chameleon exchanged places with Carleono, and with Meloni's arm looped through his, escorted her to the altar.

During the traditional nuptial Mass that followed, the service was interrupted by a unique ritual not often observed. In honor of the Blessed Virgin Mary, Meloni and the Chameleon placed an exquisite bouquet of white rose buds at the base of Mary's statue followed by a prayer led by Archbishop McKenzie.

Prior to the conclusion of Mass, Meloni and the Chameleon exchanged their sacred vows. When Archbishop McKenzie's asked the Chameleon, "Do you take this woman to be your lawfully wedded wife?" the Chameleon hesitated and shrugged his shoulders. Everyone laughed. The laughter, however, paled in comparison to the laughter that erupted from Meloni's reaction and comment that was audible to all. "It's too late to change your mind!" And, when Meloni was asked "Do you take this man to be your lawfully wedded husband?" Meloni shook her head and started to walk away. It took minutes to restore order.

The truly solemn moment came when the rings were exchanged.

"These rings represent an eternal commitment," Archbishop McKenzie announced as each placed their symbolic commitment on the finger of the other. When the Chameleon started to kiss Meloni, the Archbishop shook his head and said, "Not yet!" Again, there was loud laughter.

"For someone who couldn't make up his mind, you're sure in a hurry," Meloni whispered.

The Chameleon cringed in embarrassment and rolled his eyes.

Upon Archbishop McKenzie's pronouncement that Meloni and the Chameleon were husband and wife, the two pressed their lips together in a lingering kiss amid the thunderous applause of congratulations.

Following Archbishop McKenzie's final blessing, the newly-weds, with tears of jubilation and excited expectation, led the recessional through the length of St. Patrick's Cathedral through the main doors and out into the hopeful world that beckoned from beyond.

CHAPTER TWENTY-SEVEN

The wedding in New York was followed by a dinner and reception at Tahoe. As the crow flies, Lake Tahoe is less than twenty-four hundred miles from New York City. The flight is just a little over four hours. The preparations for the reception had started three days prior.

And, so it was, with the orchestra playing in the background and Meloni and the Chameleon standing at the head of the receiving line, guests who attended from around the globe offered their congratulations to the newly-weds.

With the ruckus surrounding them, Meloni and the Chameleon had carved out an imaginary niche or romantic cove, as they called it, to be alone together.

"Hey, Superman," Meloni said amid the din, "you seem to be adapting fairly well to all the attention."

"Since I can't avoid it, I might just as well enjoy it," the Chameleon responded, feigning intolerance and indignation.

The Chameleon's macho façade was starting to wither. For his whole life, he had for the most part, masked his feelings, starting with the death of his father. He had considered it unmanly to display his true feelings. He had demonstrated his true grit during his professional career. He had never shown any fear, apprehension or trepidation. If he had any, he kept it well hidden.

With Meloni close, Chris could smell her fragrance. Feeling her touch and gazing into her eyes, he felt the same sensation as when he met her for the very first time. He did not feel worthy of love, especially her love. She had consoled him during the wedding ceremony when he had been overcome by emotion, and now he was on the verge of turning on the waterworks once again.

"You're going to give me a complex if you keep doing that," Meloni teased while gently wiping away the tears and pressing her sweet lips against his. "I thought I made you happy."

"The only things you are missing are wings. Heaven can't get any better than this. If I am dreaming, please don't wake me. My guardian angel just materialized and contrary to superstition, she is female."

"Since my father sometimes calls me by my middle name, Angelina, and my mother by her pet name, Angel, you need to come up with your own endearment. In the interim, I will be calling you, Saint Christopher, my personal saint and my materialized guardian angel. Or, unless you object, maybe I should continue to just call you Superman."

"Just? And, in case you forgot, Saint Christopher was de-canonized."

"Don't become paranoid. You are a super man, Christopher, and I will never let you forget that. As for the de-canonization, it's just as well. I only have room in my heart for one Saint Christopher."

"Meloni, you are and will always be my great gift from God and I will never let *you* forget that, not now or ever!"

The momentary solitude was interrupted by various toasts, roasts and forays as the wedding feast at Tahoe erupted with the exuberance of a dozen Mount Saint Helens.

"I don't know where to start!" the Chameleon exclaimed as he and Meloni surveyed the appetizers beautifully arranged at the anti-pasta table.

"I only recognize a sparse few," Meloni admitted as she and the Chameleon let loose of each other's hand.

Handing the Chameleon a fine china plate gilded with gold, Meloni said, "Other than the Insalata Mare, you're on your own."

"That's the only one I'm familiar with. Guess we can't go wrong with a mixed seafood salad," the Chameleon said.

"That's the extent of my vocabulary. A lot of good it did to mark the dishes in Italian," Meloni said as she dabbed a tiny amount of Alicia Marina on her plate to taste. "This one is marinated anchovies."

The CHAMELEON

Wedging himself between the Chameleon and Meloni, Carleono pointed to the Salcicci Langostino and said, "You haven't tasted anything until you try this." He then grabbed the serving spoon and placed a hefty helping on the Chameleon's plate.

"What is it?" Meloni asked as her father placed a dab on her plate.

"Lobster sausage," he replied. Meloni's expression conveyed rejection as she grabbed the serving spoon from her father and shoved the suspect substance to the edge of her plate.

"You used to like lobster," Carleono said. "Want to try the Sarde Ripieni instead?"

"Don't tell me what it is. If I don't know, I'll be more apt to want to try it."

"Stuffed sardines is a delicacy," Carleono said. "Try it, you'll like it."

"On second thought, forget it," Meloni said as both Carleono and the Chameleon laughed.

The two had barely been seated when a waiter, dressed in a black waistcoat and wearing white gloves, started filling their wine glasses with one of the traditional Italian wines.

"What is this?" Meloni asked her father, who was now seated beside her.

"Prosecco," he responded. "It has been a tradition for weddings in the Baranetti family for generations. Yours is no exception. Everything has been designed to honor tradition and our family heritage.

Before they could take a sip, Sal, who was sitting with the wedding party at the far end of the head table, tapped his spoon on a crystal goblet. Conversation stopped and all heads pivoted toward him. He stood and raised his glass of Prosecco. "I would like to propose a toast to the bride and groom. May you live long and well. May you laugh often, love always, and grow old on one pillow."

Before the guests could respond to the toast, the Chameleon's brother, Tony, prematurely pulled a small packet of candied almonds from where the favors had been placed in front of each setting and invited the others to do likewise. Again standing and enthusiastically throwing their allotment in Meloni and the Chameleon's direction, they all shouted: *Che la vostro vita sie dolce e fruttosa* (May your life be sweet and fruitful).

The CHAMELEON

"At least now we won't have to worry about being bombarded by the Italian version of rice when we exit," Meloni whispered to the Chameleon.

"Hopefully, they used up all their ammunition," the Chameleon whispered back as the waiters emerged with the first course.

The meal began with a simple but tasty Italian wedding soup with rich, savory broth, chicken, and miniature meat balls that symbolized unity.

"The wedding soup is another Italian tradition and is thought to bring good luck," Carleono whispered to Meloni.

"It didn't work in my first marriage," Meloni whispered back.

"If it had, you wouldn't have met Chris," her father said.

Meloni arched her eyebrows. "You might say the good luck was postponed."

"Delayed but not denied," Carleono said as his and the Chameleon's eyes met.

"You didn't finish all of your soup," the Chameleon said to his new bride.

"Need to leave room for the main course," Meloni said as she nudged close to the Chameleon.

Overhearing his daughter's comment, Carleono leaned forward and said to the Chameleon, "Hope you and our guests save room for the entrées."

"I will savor each and every one . . . and a piece of our wedding cake." The Chameleon looked at Meloni and smiled.

"Attending the wedding are relatives and friends from all four regions in Italy. To honor them, our chefs have prepared dishes from each one," Carleono said.

"A good decision," replied the Chameleon as the succulent Porchetta was served. "Don't want to start your marriage out on a bad note!"

The new season in the Chameleon's life had been marked by the resolution of the mystery surrounding the death of his father and now by the marriage to the woman of his dreams. He had figuratively been to many continents, crossed many seas, looked into many eyes, heard many voices and touched many hearts. But now, he considered himself free—free from self-chastisement, self-loathing and self-pity. No longer did he consider himself to be a counterfeit, a charlatan or a man meant to be scorned. No longer was he adrift in a sea of discontent in a rudderless ship without purpose or hope. God had not only provided him with a compass and pointed him in the right direction, but literally carried him to the zenith of his life. His destiny had been forged from the beginning. Unfortunately, it had taken him two score and twelve years of twists, turns and dead ends to find out what it was. Finally, he was at peace with himself.

Meloni had selected the music for their wedding dance. It had become one of their favorite songs titled, *Can't Live Without You.* It was the perfect description of how they felt about each other. As the music began, they held each other in their arms and danced. The Chameleon pulled her closer and sang the words softly into Meloni's ear.

> *I want to spend my life with you.*
> *No one else would ever do.*
> *I'll hold you near for all eternity.*
> *Won't you come and share your life with me?*

Meloni gently pulled his earlobe with her lips then sang back to him. *Pull me close and never let me go.*

The Chameleon softly kissed her neck and whispered into her ear, "I'll never let you go—n*ever.*" He would keep that vow.

CHAPTER TWENTY-EIGHT

2010

It had been barely a year since their wedding and their honeymoon in the Bahamas. Both were, according to Adriana, still star-struck. The Chameleon had objected to the term *star struck* primarily as it applied to him and insisted that the term *shell-shocked* was by far the most descriptive. Regardless of the nomenclature, Meloni and the Chameleon were without question leading a Camelot existence and loving every minute.

It was July fourth, two thousand ten, with the Chicago temperature reaching a sweltering ninety degrees. This year, the Chameleon and Meloni didn't have to drive to Sal's Fourth of July Extravaganza. They were within walking distance, thanks to the generous wedding gift of a house from the Baranettis. The house was not quite as

316

elegant as Lenna and Sal's, but it was lovely and spacious nonetheless. The feature that had impressed the Chameleon the most was the separate mother-in-law quarters. Even before becoming aware of the phenomenal wedding gift, Meloni and the Chameleon had already discussed asking Adriana to move in with them.

The Carcellis' lived just around the corner from Sal and Lenna. With the Chameleon flanked by his wife and mother, the trio strolled arm in arm down the boulevard. Adriana insisted they arrive early so they could help with the preparations.

Because of the Chameleon's intense demands at the CPD, he was finding himself compromised somewhat by his personal interests and conflicted by the time demands of each. Since he had started working with the Baranettis' family corporations, it was obvious that he was being groomed for directorship. His focus was changing so much that he was experiencing guilt over abandoning a career that had, up to this point, satisfied him. All knew it wouldn't be long before the Chameleon would become Carleono's alter ego. In fact, each day he was growing closer to the inevitable.

Although his duties as head of the detective squad with the CPD were challenging and he welcomed the ability to be the chief decision maker, he missed the field, particularly working undercover. The most valuable assets of an undercover agent were measured by daring, courage, persistence and success. Regardless, being an administrator was like being a coach. The Chameleon missed being part of the action and was not content with just being on the sidelines.

The Chameleon had played city-league basketball with an attorney who became a trial judge then promptly returned to being a trial attorney. Curious about why the attorney abdicated the judicial "throne" and all the power and prestige that went with it, he confronted him.

"Trials are like athletic events," his friend responded. "They are the purest form of competition. Wins and losses in murder cases, unlike sporting contests, for example, can dictate who lives and who dies. Judges are like referees.

318

They just make sure the game is played by the rules. They are, for all intents and purposes, traffic cops. Would you want to be a player directly involved in the excitement of the game, or would you rather be an umpire, referee or traffic cop and just direct traffic?"

The Chameleon understood only too well the difference between being directly involved and being peripherally involved in his work. The players were certainly an extension of the coach but it was clear his vicarious involvement as an administrator was not satisfying, not to him nor to his department. The Chameleon longed to return to the action. Yet, in his career, he had reached the point of diminishing return, or more aptly, the point of no return.

The previous month, the Chameleon had received his thirty-year pin commemorating his years of service with the CPD. He was sworn in at the age of twenty-two and was now fifty-two. It was bittersweet knowing that he had already outlived his father by almost two decades. He remembered thinking his father was old as he watched his father blow out the thirty-three candles on his last birthday cake. That was over a half century ago. Now, he was wondering how many candles he would be blowing out before he joined his father.

The thought of retirement from the CPD had soon become a preoccupation. The exciting new lure of the business world was beckoning. He knew he could not succumb just yet because he still had to contend with some police business that remained unfinished.

EPILOGUE

_____

2010

It had been almost four years since Vincenti Bari Mazzini's staged burial in Our Lady of Lourdes Cemetery in Golden, Colorado, had taken place. As far as Marcus Sagibaro and his crime family were concerned, the man they knew by that name or simply as "Vinnie" had gone to meet his maker. That perception had persisted despite the celebrity status conferred on the Chameleon on the east coast as a result of his heroic exploits. Sagibaro and his cronies had been too preoccupied to connect the dots.

At the time Vinnie was laid to rest, Sagibaro and his band of thugs, feeling the heat and wanting to distance themselves, reputedly fled to South America. Although it was thought that Sagibaro's new staging area was a Colombian port along the Pacific Ocean, it was never confirmed. It was more likely that he operated out of Bolivia since government intelligence had reported confirmed sightings of members of his immediate family in that locale. Again, his presence there was pure speculation, as he was never seen in or around the area. In fact, he seemed to have disappeared from the face of the earth.

With his international ties, Sagibaro could have been holed up anywhere on the planet. It was obvious that he had been forewarned of the peril of his North American operations; otherwise he would not have withdrawn in such haste. His claim, as it turned out, that he had tentacles in high places, apparently had some validity.

In March of 2010, Sagibaro returned to the United States and boldly reclaimed his old territory in Golden, feeling he could operate inconspicuously there. It was obvious he was aware of his organization's weak link as a key government informant disappeared shortly after his return. The state prosecution of Sagibaro on the murder conspiracy case involving the Chameleon had been put on hold at the request of the feds so that the latter could put together a RICO prosecution. Unfortunately, the much-needed evidence never materialized. And, with the unavailability of the key witness, the fed's case disintegrated.

There was a three-year statute of limitations in Colorado on most felonies, which meant charges were required to have been filed no later than September of 2009. Fortunately, there was no statute of limitations on first degree murder or first degree kidnapping. Therefore, murder charges in the deaths of Carl "Bull" Cosconi and Ivoni "Twitch" Baratoli and the kidnapping of Vincenti Bari Mazzini could be filed at any time. Under the felony murder rule, if someone was killed during the commission of a felony, all those connected with the crime could be charged with murder. That meant, Sagibaro could be charged in the deaths of his two henchmen but not in the conspiracy involving the ordered death of the Chameleon.

That Sagibaro was a great escape artist and able to cover his tracks or literally bury the evidence was undeniable. Watchful waiting no longer was considered to be an effective strategy. And, so with little corroborative evidence, the possible conviction of Sagibaro and his removal from society rested squarely upon the shoulders of the Chameleon. It would be his testimony that would either make or break the case of *The People of the State of Colorado versus Marcus Sagibaro.*

Jury selection had begun on the Monday of the second full week in September of 2010. Jury selection was somewhat cumbersome in light of the fact that the state was asking for the death penalty and the defendant was claiming that the jury pool had been tainted as a result of the prospective jurors having been exposed to massive and pervasive prejudicial pretrial publicity.

It was indisputable that the arrest of Sagibaro and his subsequent prosecution garnered the attention of the local media outlets. However, whether it tainted prospective jurors to favor the prosecution or the defendant had yet to be determined. The idea of a mobster in their midst had attracted a sizable group of the curious who crowded into the courtroom.

The prosecuting attorney assigned the case was a chief trial deputy by the name of Rhoda Claxton, a petite, unimposing woman in her late forties. Though her features were delicate, her demeanor wasn't. Her eyes were probing and in trial she had the tenacity and ferocity of a mother cat that had just given birth to kittens. Once she had her opponent pinned against the wall, the prey was at her mercy. Experienced and gifted, she was relentless in seeking a conviction. With her win-loss record what it was, one might have expected that she was only prosecuting the slam-dunks. In reality, the opposite was true.

Rhoda had a formable opponent in Horatio (Horace) Kensington. Approaching retirement age, Horace was bent upon upholding his record as a dragon slayer. With a long marshmallow-white beard and thick matching head of hair tied in a ponytail, he might have been mistaken for Santa Claus. That is until you encountered his cruel piercing eyes. Then, you knew you would be ill-advised to cross him or attempt to do so.

Horace had the reputation of improvising. The district attorney's office had a different term to describe his talent: manufacturing evidence. To say that Horace was slippery might be perceived as patronizing by his

325

detractors. By his fans, however, he was described as cunning and shrewd. Regardless, his office was filled with a wall of scalps. Rhoda would be guarding her flanks and be trial-ready. Her scalp would not be on Horace's wall if she could help it.

The first week of trial was fairly uneventful and consisted mainly of *voir dire,* or the jury selection process. To some it was boring and to others it was enlightening. To the attorneys, it was perhaps the most critical phase of the trial. The outcome would depend on the caliber of the jurors selected. Once the jury was sworn in, the litigants would live or die by their decision. That was literally the case here where the death penalty was at issue.

On the morning of the start of the second week, Judge Coleman Collier swore in the trial jurors and advised them of the nature of the charges. "Marcus Sagibaro is charged with two counts of felony murder in the deaths of Carl Cosconi and Ivoni Beratoli and one count of kidnapping wherein Vincenti Bari Mazzini is the named victim."

Judge Collier examined the charge form. "The events are alleged to have occurred in this county on September 15, 2006."

Pausing and peering over his steel rimmed eye glasses, he asked, "Mrs. Claxton, is the prosecution ready to proceed with its opening statement?"

"We are, your honor," Rhoda said as she tore a single handwritten page from her yellow legal pad and walked determinedly to the podium.

Scanning the jury, Rhoda began in a subdued voice, "Good morning ladies and gentlemen. I am Rhoda Claxton, the prosecutor in this case. It is my job to present the facts proving the allegations contained in the charge form. Bear in mind that the opening statements are not evidence. They are nothing more than an outline of the evidence each side expects to present. The evidence itself will come from the sworn statements of witnesses.

"Since the prosecution has the burden of proving the guilt of Marcus Sagibaro, the defendant in this case, beyond a reasonable doubt, we go first. We will be calling a number of witnesses who will be establishing the following:

"An undercover agent using the alias of Vincenti Bari Mazzini had infiltrated an organization run by the defendant. Upon discovering that Mazzini was a government operative, the defendant slit his throat with a stiletto, but not enough to kill him, and ordered two of his henchmen, Carl 'Bull' Cosconi and Ivoni 'Twitch' Beratoli to execute Mazzini.

"While traveling on Highway 6 West in the direction of Central City, the vehicle owned by the defendant veered out of control and tumbled into a rocky ravine. All three of the occupants, Cosconi, Beratoli and Mazzini, were initially declared dead at the scene.

"You'll be instructed by Judge Collier at the conclusion of all of the evidence, that if such facts are proven to your satisfaction beyond a reasonable doubt, you must find Marcus Sagibaro, the defendant in this case, guilty of two counts of felony murder and one count of kidnapping, all Class 1 felonies.

"If the evidence is produced as I expect it to be, I will have no hesitancy at the conclusion of the case in asking you to return three guilty verdicts."

Rhoda retrieved the handwritten sheet from the podium and, returning to the prosecution's table, placed it in one of her folders.

CARROLL MULTZ

Horace snickered as Rhoda folded her arms and stared straight ahead. Whispering to Sagibaro, he said, "She still doesn't realize that the DA's Office forgot to include Mazzini in the murder charges."

Sagibaro arched his eyebrows and whispered back, "So what else is new?"

"Mr. Kensington," Judge Collier said impatiently, "Do you intend to make an opening statement now or reserve it?"

Horace took his time in responding and, collecting his legal pad and several folders, ambled to the podium.

Without addressing the jury, Horace, in a scratchy voice, began, "Excuse the voice. I woke up this way this morning. Hopefully, you can all hear me." Not all the jurors nodded.

"My client is not guilty of any wrongdoing. Carl Cosconi, Ivoni Beratoli and Vinnie Mazzini all worked for Marcus. He cared about all his employees. Ivoni was married to Marcus' sister, Maria. Vinnie was Marcus' bookkeeper.

"At the time of the fatal crash, Marcus was not present and only became aware of the accident sometime after the fact. The circumstances remain a mystery. The deaths of the three were listed on the CSP and coroner's reports as accidental.

"The only nexus Marcus had to the accident was his ownership of the vehicle they were driving. The vehicle was less than a year old and there was no indication that it was defective or faulty or that it had been tampered with in any way."

Whether for effect or necessity, Horace searched his pockets for a lozenge. Sensing the dilemma, one of his associates brought one to the podium along with a glass of water. Taking a gulp of water and placing the lozenge in his mouth, he continued.

"As the prosecutor has said, they have the burden of proving my client's guilt beyond a reasonable doubt. Not only is the prosecution required to prove a criminal act but the culpable mental state as well. That means that even if they prove some criminal act, that would not be enough for a conviction. To succeed in a first degree murder prosecution, there has to be proof beyond a reasonable doubt that the act was done deliberately."

Rhoda sprung to her feet. "Objection. This is an opening statement not a final argument. Besides, the prosecution here is based on the felony murder rule. Mr. Kensington's statement, therefore, is contrary to the law applicable in this case."

"Sustained. Mr. Kensington, this is not final argument." Judge Collier then turned to the jury. "Ladies and gentlemen, you are to disregard defense counsel's reference to the law that he thinks should apply in this case. I will instruct you on the law once all the evidence is in."

Turning to Horace, he said, "Anything further, Mr. Kensington?"

"No, your honor," Horace said without so much as even an apology.

Rhoda was then instructed by Judge Collier to present the prosecution's case-in-chief.

Rhoda's presentation was mechanical and methodical. By week's end she had succeeded in presenting all the crime scene and forensic evidence, including that of the investigating officers, the pathologist and the toxicologist. It was a rather brisk trial, considering Horace's redundancy and belabored and ineffective cross-examination.

On the last Monday of September, there was excitement in the air as Rhoda announced that the prosecution was calling its last witness. Because the sequestration rule was in effect, which prevented all but the testifying witness to be in the courtroom, witnesses awaited their turn either in the hall or special witness rooms adjacent to the hall. During the prosecution's case-in-chief, only the prosecutor knew for certain who was to be called next.

The configuration of the courtroom was typical, with the presiding judge elevated above everyone else facing the double doors to the courtroom. The jury box was at a ninety-degree angle, which also allowed an unfettered view of the double doors. Inside the railing surrounding the judge and his aides and the jury box were two large oak counsel tables on either side, both facing the judge with the backs of the chairs facing the double-doors. The spectators' benches also had their backs to the double doors.

The counsel table closest to the jury box was designated the prosecution's table; the other, the defense's table. Seated at the defense table with their backs to the double doors were Sagibaro's attorney and Sagibaro. The two apparently had been lulled into a false sense of security by what they must have considered to be a dearth of evidence. With only one witness left to be called by the prosecution, the defense was already smelling an acquittal.

The swagger and arrogance of defense attorneys is legend, particularly at that stage when they think they have the case in the bag. The defendant and his attorney seemed rather smug and smirked at each other when Rhoda announced that the prosecution was calling Vincenti Bari Mazzini to the stand. They were the only ones who did not turn to watch as Vincenti Bari Mazzini, also known as Christopher Claudio Carcelli and the Chameleon, entered the courtroom.

It wasn't until the Chameleon walked to the front of the courtroom, was administered the oath and took the stand that Sagibaro realized that the key witness he thought was dead was very much alive. Sagibaro slumped in his chair as he stared into the eyes of the man whose execution he had ordered. It was not a stare-down. If it had been, the Chameleon would have won the contest, as it was only Sagibaro who flinched. Sagibaro grew ashen and the look in his eyes made one wonder if maybe Sagibaro thought he was staring into the face of a ghost. The Chameleon watched as Sagibaro frantically surveyed the courtroom, apparently searching for a place to hide or an exit from which to flee. For long moments, Sagibaro seemed frozen in space with consternation etched on his face. Sagibaro was no longer the predator but the prey. It was obvious he was in the midst of a meltdown—one from which he would never recover.

In Colorado, the prosecution was required to list or endorse potential witnesses. Those who were not so listed or endorsed could not be called. Rhoda had included in the prosecution's list of witnesses the names of the three victims specifically, Carl Cosconi, Ivoni Beratoli and Vincenti Bari Mazzini. Believing that the three were deceased, the defense had obviously not attempted to interview them nor had Horace filed a motion for disclosure of the aliases of the witnesses so endorsed.

Thinking there were no eye-witnesses to the incident, Horace at trial was not aggressive in seeking to exclude evidence seized at the scene of the fatal crash. It was Horace's strategy to appear not to be hiding anything and allow all the "harmless" items to be admitted. In his thinking, none pointed to any criminal agency on the part of his client.

"Would you state your full name to the jury?" Rhoda asked.

"Christopher Claudio Carcelli," the Chameleon replied.

Horace leapt to his feet as though he had been stung by a hornet. "Objection," he shouted.

"Ms. Claxton, only asked the witness his name," Judge Collier said with a frown.

"Your honor," Horace persisted, "this witness has not been endorsed!"

"Ms. Claxton?" Judge Collier said as he removed his glasses and pointed them in Rhoda's direction.

"We were not given an opportunity to lay a foundation," Rhoda said.

"Very well, proceed. I will reserve ruling on the objection."

"Do you go by any other name?" Rhoda asked the Chameleon.

"Yes. During the time of law enforcement's investigation of Marcus Sagibaro, I went by the name of Vincenti Bari Mazzini."

When Horace started to rise, Judge Collier motioned for him to remain seated.

"Did you have a driver's license in that name?" Rhoda asked.

"Yes," the Chameleon replied.

"How about a Social Security card in that name?"

"Yes."

"Credit cards?"

"Yes."

"Business cards?"

"Yes. All were in my undercover name. For all intents and purposes, I was Vincenti Bari Mazzini."

"Did you have a nickname?"

"Yes, I was called Vinnie."

Rhoda then looked at Judge Collier. "That completes my foundational questions."

"Do you still persist in your objection?" Judge Collier asked Horace.

"Absolutely," Horace said as he stood flushed and ready to do battle. "Although Vincenti Bari Mazzini was endorsed as a witness, Christopher Claudio Carcelli was not. Therefore, the Rules preclude him from testifying."

Judge Collier looked at Horace and shook his head. "In going through the file, I don't see anything filed by the defense seeking the assumed names or aliases of the endorsed witnesses. Am I missing something?"

Horace was so enraged that he just sat down and stared at Judge Collier. All the while, Sagibaro glared at Horace. One could only surmise what Sagibaro must have been thinking in light of the Chameleon's anticipated testimony.

"For the record, Mr. Kensington, your objection is overruled." Directing his remarks at Rhoda, he said, "Ms. Claxton, you may continue with your examination of this witness."

"What is your occupation?"

"I am a detective with the Chicago Police Department."

"How long have you been so employed?"

"I just recently received my thirty year pin."

"In September of 2006 and, for some time prior thereto, were you on loan to the Denver Police Department?"

"I was."

"And, for what purpose?"

"A freight company owned by Marcus Sagibaro was thought to be involved in illegal drug distribution. I was brought in as an unfamiliar face to infiltrate Mr. Sagibaro's operations. Therefore, I sought employment by Mr. Sagibaro."

"Did he hire you?"

"Yes."

"How long were you so employed?"

"Close to six months."

"What was your position?"

"I was Mr. Sagibaro's bookkeeper."

"Were you considered his confidant, as well?"

"He confided in me in both business and personal matters."

"On September 14, 2006, did something disrupt your relationship with Mr. Sagibaro?"

"Yes. He discovered a transponder on the underside of his limo and a similar device in the bottom of my gym bag."

"What did he do?"

"He tied me to a chair and slashed my throat with a stiletto and said, 'You just earned a death warrant.'"

"Did he say anything further?"

"He called me a traitor and said I would never be able to snitch on him or anyone else again."

"What did he do next?"

"He called in two of his toughs, Carl 'Bull' Cosconi and Ivoni 'Twitch' Beratoli and ordered them to execute me."

"Did the two proceed to do so?"

"Early the following morning, Bull untied me and he and Twitch placed me in Mr. Sagibaro's Chrysler 300 SRT8 and Bull proceeded to drive west on Highway 6 out of Denver."

"Did either of the two say what they intended to do once you reached your destination?"

"Yes. Twitch said they were taking me to his brother-in-law's favorite cemetery."

"And, who was Twitch's brother-in-law?"

"Marcus Sagibaro."

"What then occurred?"

"After a brief distance, we were stopped in traffic while a road crew cleared some rock. Just outside the construction zone, I was able to remove my belt and wrap it around Bull's neck. This caused the vehicle to career off of the road and into a deep ravine. I don't remember anything after that except waking up in a hospital room ten days later. It was then I learned Bull and Twitch had been killed in the crash."

Both Sagibaro and his attorney squirmed in their chairs. Sagibaro avoided making eye contact with the Chameleon.

"Did the knife wound to which you testified leave a scar?"

"Yes."

"Would you point out the scar to the jury, please?" Rhoda then looked to Judge Collier for approval.

Judge Collier nodded and said, "He will be permitted to do so."

The Chameleon rose and walked to the front of the jury box. Opening up his shirt and spreading the collar, he said, "This is the scar that was caused when Mr. Sagibaro slashed my throat."

Several of the female jurors gasped and looked away. One of the jurors had tears in her eyes. Sagibaro looked off into the opposite direction.

After the Chameleon returned to the witness chair, Rhoda retrieved a handkerchief containing dried blood that had already been introduced into evidence. "I hand you People's Exhibit 118 and ask if you can identify it?"

"That is my handkerchief, one that I held against my neck to stop the bleeding after I was placed in Mr. Sagibaro's Chrysler."

"You are referring to the knife wound inflicted by the defendant on the previous day?"

"Yes."

"How do you know this handkerchief is one and the same?"

"It has my initials monogramed on it, VBM, and dried blood."

The Chameleon held up the handkerchief and pointed to his initials.

Rhoda retrieved a wallet found at the crime scene that also had been identified by one of the prior witnesses. "I hand you People's Exhibit 119 and ask if you can identify it?"

The Chameleon examined the wallet and its contents. "This is the wallet I had when I was being transported by Bull and Twitch."

"How do you know it is one and the same?"

"I recognize the wallet and the contents which consist of my driver's license, my Social Security card, three of my credit cards and several of my business cards."

"Can you identify the man you knew and referred to in your testimony as Marcus Sagibaro, the man who had ordered your execution and the man who carved his death warrant on your throat?"

"Yes."

"Would you point him out to the jury, please?"

Alighting from his witness chair and marching with determination to the defense table where Sagibaro sat quivering, the Chameleon pointed his imposing right index finger in Sagibaro's face, almost touching Sagibaro's prominent nose, and said, "This is the man!"

342

Striking the gavel against the polished oak top in front of him, Judge Collier growled, "Sir, that type of conduct is not permitted in this courtroom. Please immediately return to the witness stand."

The Chameleon did as Judge Collier ordered. There was no smile on the Chameleon's face as he took his seat and glared at Sagibaro.

The Chameleon's testimony was devastating and even Horace was disgusted with himself over his ineptness on cross-examination to shake the Chameleon or put a chink in his armor. Rattled, Horace aborted his cross-examination in mid-stream and dejectedly retreated to the defense table. Horace and his client reminded the Chameleon of two of his eighth-grade buddies whom he had observed sitting in the principal's office after they had been caught smoking at recess.

Rhoda announced that the prosecution rested its case-in-chief. Horace made a half-hearted effort in moving for dismissal on what he called "insufficiency of the evidence." That, of course, was denied and now it was time for the defendant's case-in-chief.

The CHAMELEON

After a brief recess, Horace announced, "The defendant will rest on his presumption of innocence. Because of his right not to have to present evidence and mainly in light of the scanty evidence presented by the prosecution, Mr. Sagibaro, upon my advice, has elected to rest his case-in-chief."

After the judge instructed the jury on the law, Rhoda and Horace made their final arguments.

Rhoda went first. "Ladies and gentlemen of the jury, we thank you for sitting as jurors in this case. The role jurors play in deliberating and returning a verdict is the most crucial feature of a criminal jury trial. You are now called upon to evaluate the evidence in light of the law as contained in the jury instructions.

"In my opening statement, I told you that if the evidence presented was as I anticipated, I would have no hesitancy at the conclusion of the case in asking you to return three guilty verdicts. It was as I anticipated. Now I'm asking you to return those guilty verdicts.

"The undisputed evidence is as follows: The death vehicle was registered in the defendant's name. At the time of their fateful journey, all three of the victims, Carl Cosconi, Ivoni Beratoli and Vincenti Mazzini were employees of the defendant. The defendant had ordered Casconi and Beratoli to execute Mazzini. They were on their way to do so at the time of the fatal crash.

"The weapons found in the tangled wreckage were registered to the defendant. Toll records for the defendant's cellphone confirmed the communication between him and his two henchmen during the journey to their deaths. The blood-soaked handkerchief Mazzini held to his throat as a result of the defendant's goodbye gesture was recovered from the wreckage and analyzed. Mazzini's blood splattered wallet with his identification was also recovered from the wreckage. Both items were determined to contain the blood of Mazzini, thus corroborating Mazzini's testimony with regard to the defendant's wrath and ordered execution.

"There is enough circumstantial evidence to convict even without the eyewitness testimony of one of the victims."

Now it was Horace's turn. "Ladies and gentlemen, the only evidence that transforms an otherwise innocent trip in the mountains into a criminal act is the testimony of an undercover agent who is trained to lie and deceive. Unfortunately, Carl Cosconi and Ivoni Beratoli are not here to tell their side of the story. What their intentions were is mere speculation. Remember, from the jury instructions given you by the judge, you can't convict on speculation.

"Because Marcus was the registered owner of the vehicle involved in the fatal crash, he is on trial for the murder of his two employees. This is despite the fact that the reports of the Colorado State Patrol and the coroner list the cause of death as accidental. Now, the prosecution is attempting to elevate the cause of death to murder. Did any of you hear any evidence to the effect that Marcus wanted either Carl or Ivoni dead? I didn't. Mazzini is no worse for wear. He sports a scratch on his neck that could very easily have come from the accident. It is only his word that the scar came from another source.

"That leaves us with the kidnap charge which is just as bogus. It wasn't Mazzini's ghost who testified at this trial. And, the fact that the prosecution waited almost four years to bring criminal charges tells you something. To show you how desperate the police are to convict Marcus, they even dummied up the reports listing Mazzini as a fatality. The prosecution's case is thus fraught with contradictions—enough to make their case and motives suspect.

"If the prosecution entertained doubt about their case and waited almost four years to bring charges, it is no wonder then that you would have the same doubt. Just because criminal charges have been filed against Marcus doesn't mean they're meritorious. And, just because Carcelli alias Mazzini claims he was kidnapped doesn't make it so. The jury instructions read to you by Judge Collier tell you to use common sense in arriving at a verdict. I'm asking you to do the same thing.

"Serious charges require serious deliberation. Serious deliberation exposes serious doubt. And, serious doubt requires an acquittal. Don't base a conviction on a paid governmental operative who is trained to out-con the cons. Justice would not be served by a conviction in this case. The only fair verdicts are verdicts of not guilty."

"Any rebuttal, Ms. Claxton?" the judge asked.

"Only briefly, Your Honor. Ladies and gentlemen, whether the defendant wished only the death of Vincenti Mazzini and not of the defendant's two henchmen is immaterial. The felony murder rule does not require intent to kill on the part of the defendant only the occurrence of death during the commission of a crime in which the defendant participated. The evidence both direct and circumstantial is overwhelming. Remember, Mr. Kensington's statements are not evidence. The only evidence presented in this case is evidence of the defendant's guilt."

Because of the lateness in the day, the trial was recessed to the following day at which time the jury would commence its deliberations. In less than four hours, the jury had reached a unanimous verdict.

Fifteen minutes before noon on Thursday, the thirtieth day of September, and four years almost to the day of the fatal excursion, Sagibaro was convicted of two counts of first-degree murder and one count of first-degree kidnapping, all capital offenses.

The Chameleon testified at the penalty phase of the trial, as did Sagibaro. For a man who had been heartless and deaf to the pleas of mercy from his victims, it was paradoxical now to watch Sagibaro plead for mercy in his own behalf. Sagibaro's plea, however, fell on deaf ears. The jury in less than one hour of deliberation voted for imposition of the death penalty.

Though Sagibaro's conviction and particularly his death sentence would have to run its course through the appellate process, Sagibaro got as good as he gave. It was not the criminal justice system that had sealed his fate, it was him.

Meloni and the Chameleon had enjoyed their time together in Denver. They visited the museum, aquarium and historical sites. They even enjoyed the gaming tables at Central City, not far from the site of the fateful car crash in 2006, and their brief visit to Glenwood Springs where they rafted down the Colorado River. They would be spending the weekend in Moab, Utah, and return to Glenwood Springs before flying back to Chicago on that following Monday.

It was difficult to imagine a time without Meloni, and the Chameleon had followed his mother's advice in resetting his priorities. It had taken over a half-century to do so. Wisdom, he found was not in not making mistakes but in learning from them. *The Lamb's Book of Life* would now be adding still another name to the Chameleon's long list of aliases: *The Wiseman* (wise man).

About the Author

Carroll Multz has authored or co-authored twelve books and technical manuals. This is his fifth novel. A trial lawyer for over forty years, a former two-term district attorney, assistant attorney general, and judge, he has been involved in cases ranging from municipal courts to and including the United States Supreme Court. Multz's high profile cases have been reported in the *New York Times, Redbook Magazine* and various police magazines. He was one of the attorneys in the Columbine Copycat Case that occurred in Fort Collins, Colorado in 2001 that was featured by Barbara Walters on ABC's *20/20*. Now retired, Multz is an Adjunct Professor at Colorado Mesa University in Grand Junction, Colorado, teaching law-related courses at both the graduate and undergraduate levels.